MAPLE GROVE

Richard Telesca

dizzyemupublishing.com

DIZZY EMU PUBLISHING

1714 N McCadden Place, Hollywood, Los Angeles 90028

dizzyemupublishing.com

Maple Grove
Richard Telesca

First published in the United States
in 2022 by Dizzy Emu Publishing

dizzyemupublishing.com

MAPLE GROVE

Richard Telesca

MAPLE GROVE

FADE IN:

1   EXT. JAPAN 1945 - PACIFIC OCEAN - DAY   1

     SUPER: TOKYO 1945

     Just off the coast of Japan a sea battle rages as Japanese
     aircraft attack the U.S. fleet.

     A Japanese Zero "Kamikaze" aircraft circles high over the
     fleet and starts its dive on a U.S. aircraft carrier.
     Withering fire from the carrier and escort ships does not
     slow it down, and the carrier appears doomed for a direct
     hit.

     Suddenly, a U.S. Navy F4U Corsair braves the wall of friendly
     fire and climbs towards the Zero with guns blazing, but it
     also fails to stop the Kamikaze's assault.

     A RADIO OPERATOR from the Carrier tries to warn the pilot in
     the Corsair.

                         RADIO OPERATOR (V.O.)
                    Roost to Raven one, Roost to Raven
                    one. You are entering an active
                    fire zone. Roll out.

     The pilot of the Corsair does not respond. The Radio Operator
     tries again with more urgency as the Corsair is ripped by
     friendly fire from the ships below.

                         RADIO OPERATOR (V.O.) (CONT'D)
                    Roost to Raven one, Roost to Raven
                    one. You are entering an active
                    fire zone. Roll out! Roll out,
                    Raven one!

     The crew of the carrier watch in awe as the pilot of the
     Corsair broadsides the tail of the Zero with his plane. The
     Zero breaks in half and plunges into the ocean. The Corsair,
     heavily damaged, climbs for a moment, and then noses down
     and crashes into the sea.

2   EXT. MAIN STREET (ROUTE 66) MAPLE GROVE, ILLINOIS - DAY   2

     SUPER: 8 YEARS LATER

     Maple Grove, Illinois, is a typical 1950's era American small
     town with an old-fashioned, tree-lined Main Street that runs
     along Route 66. Side by side on Main Street are the
     traditional drug store, mom and pop shops, bank, barber shop,
     hardware store, and Vivian's Bake Shop etc. At night the
     street lights up with the glowing colors of neon signs.

                                                        (CONTINUED)

Main Street is decorated for the 4th of July with bunting
and American flags. Banners announce the Annual 4th of July
Celebration.

VIVIAN'S BAKE SHOP

The shop is a simple brick building with an awning and a
large window to the right of the front door. An "OPEN" sign
hangs on the door.

3   INT. VIVIAN'S BAKE SHOP - MAIN STREET   3

VIVIAN DONNELLY sits near the front window at one of 3 small
cafe tables and chats with her friend and sometimes employee
CLARICE. Both wear pink, pin-striped dresses with white,
ruffled bibbed aprons.

Vivian is late twenties and a longhaired, blue-eyed blonde
who is the personification of a 1940's pin up girl. Her
cover girl looks conceal the enigma that is Vivian; a smart
businesswoman and master of her craft torn between her
professional ambition and her desire to escape the past and
find true love.

                    VIVIAN
          I just don't know what kind of future
          I have here anymore.

                    CLARICE
          Bryce isn't so bad, and he's
          successful. You could do a lot worse.

Vivian nods, but her expression reveals she is unconvinced.

                    VIVIAN
          Maybe it's time for a change. I
          could move to St. Louis, or Chicago.
          Maybe somebody there would be
          interested in my bakery idea.

                    CLARICE
          What about your sister and little
          Eddie? They love you!

Vivian smiles. They are the bright spot in her life.

                    CLARICE (CONT'D)
               (facetiously)
          Maybe, you can be rich and miserable!
               (a beat)
          What's bothering you is on the inside.
          Moving away won't help.

Clarice clasps Vivian's hands in hers.

                                        (CONTINUED)

                    CLARICE (CONT'D)
               (gently)
          It's been 8 years. Let it go.

4   EXT. NEW YORK CITY - SIMULTANEOUS   4

     The bustling Metropolis hums with activity as scores of people
     and TRAFFIC rush through the canyons of skyscrapers.

5   INT. CORPORATE OFFICE OF SCOTT ENTERPRISES - NEW YORK CITY   5

     TOMMY BOYD searches the office for RICK "SCOTTY" SCOTT with
     a telegram in hand and no success. Exasperated, he sits on
     a desk in frustration.

     Scotty breezes in dressed in baggy khaki cargo pants, a khaki
     shirt and a well-preserved brown, lightweight WWII Leather
     flight jacket. He is early thirties with dark wavy hair.

     Scotty is an MIT educated engineer and WW II Navy veteran.
     He exhibits the manners of an officer and a gentleman, which
     belie the little boy inside hoping to reconnect with the
     simple life of his youth.

                    TOMMY
          I've been looking for you! You've
          been M-I-A a lot lately.

                    SCOTTY
          Had some things to do.

     Tommy tweaks the collar of the leather jacket.

                    TOMMY
          You've been out flying again! I'm
          sorry about your mom, but you have
          to focus on business!

                    SCOTTY
          C'mon Tommy. I'm just not cut out
          for the corporate lifestyle.

                    TOMMY
          OK, OK. You're worn out. What say
          we call the girls, go out and have a
          few laughs.

                    SCOTTY
          Yeah, I'm tired. Tired of this city,
          tired of the city night life, tired
          of all the constant traffic and noise.

                    TOMMY
          What's your problem?
               (MORE)

                                        (CONTINUED)

                    TOMMY (CONT'D)
          You've become a rich man. The owner
          of a very prosperous corporation.
          Enjoy it!

Scotty dismisses Tommy's admonishment with a shake of his
head.

                    TOMMY (CONT'D)
          You're not going to find what you're
          looking for in the clouds. Face it!
          That small town world is in your
          past!

Scotty just stares at him, pondering that wisdom.

                    TOMMY (CONT'D)
          Anyway, the plans for the new office
          in L.A. are all set. One of us has
          to be out there by August first.

Scotty does not respond.

                    TOMMY (CONT'D)
          You hate this city so much, you go.

Scotty is reluctant at first, but then begins to nod slowly.

                    SCOTTY
          OK, I'll go, but I'm gonna drive.

                    TOMMY
          You're crazy.

                    SCOTTY
          You just said...

                    TOMMY
          --I know what I just said, but...

                    SCOTTY
          --That I won't find what I'm looking
          for in the clouds. OK then.

                    TOMMY
          Scotty, you can't go home again!
          That small town life passed with
          your mom and dad. It's a new world.

Scotty responds with a grin. But that only makes Tommy
uneasy.

                    SCOTTY
          I'll take my chances. I got 30 days
          to get there. What could go wrong?

                                        (CONTINUED)

Scotty takes the telegram. Tommy takes a deep breath and exhales sharply.

6   EXT. SMALLTOWN, CONNECTICUT - MORNING - DAYS LATER -   6
        SATURDAY, JUNE 27, 1953

Scotty stops his 1952 Chevrolet Convertible outside a small ranch-style house on a quiet street. A "SOLD" sign hangs out front. Nearby, children play baseball on an empty lot.

Scotty steps out of the car and leans against the front fender. He pulls an old photo from his pocket.

INSERT PHOTO

of Scotty as a young boy posing with his parents in front of the house.

BACK TO SCENE

Scotty looks at the children, and then the house, wistfully. He gets back into the car and drives off.

7   EXT. SCOTTY'S CAR - MOMENTS LATER   7

Scotty turns the car onto a road and passes a route sign.

INSERT SIGN

which is a US Highway Route shield that reads "Connecticut US 6 WEST".

BACK TO SCENE

The car disappears down the highway.

8   EXT. ROUTE 6   8

SERIES OF SHOTS

over two and a half days as Scotty travels US Route 6 West from Connecticut to Joliet, Illinois. Long days with

-- US State Route 6 Signs in New York, Pennsylvania, Ohio, Indiana

-- Billboards

-- Diners, Drive Ins

-- Gas Stations

-- Overnight Motels

                                        (CONTINUED)

-- Scotty passes a Welcome to Illinois sign on Monday, June 29, 1953.

BACK TO SCENE

Scotty turns onto Route 66 West in Joliet, Illinois.

9   INT. SCOTTY'S CAR - LATE AFTERNOON   9

Scotty passes a sign on Route 66.

INSERT SIGN

which reads, Maple Grove 3 Miles

BACK TO SCENE

Scotty checks his watch. He turns on the radio and hears only STATIC. He adjusts the radio and finds a MUSIC station out of St. Louis.

10   EXT. SCOTTY'S CAR   10

The car SPUTTERS and STALLS. Scotty gets it running, but only gets about a mile or two before it SPUTTERS and STALLS again.

11   EXT. MAPLE GROVE GAS STATION - MAIN STREET   11

Scotty manages to roll into the Maple Grove Gas Station, a white building that sits adjacent to the Maple Grove Motor Court on the edge of town.

Scotty tries to restart the car, but no luck. He steps out and looks around.

The Maple Grove Motor Court is a motel with 10 separate guest cabins that sit atop a gentle hill on a circular driveway; a Coffee/Sandwich Shop connected to the motel office; and, the gas station on one corner. A large green with a swimming pool separates the cabins from the highway.

A grove of Maple trees sits just behind the motel on one end of the property.

Scotty is greeted by the gas station attendant, CARL, an old black man dressed in gray herringbone coveralls.

                    CARL
          Can I help you, sir?

                    SCOTTY
          Darn thing quit on me. Can't seem
          to get it started.

                              (CONTINUED)

Carl looks at the car and scratches his head.

                    CARL
          Sorry sir. You'll have to talk to
          Mr. Hanke. He does all the fixin'
          around here.

Scotty waits for further directions, but Carl just nods as
he looks over the car.

                    SCOTTY
          So, where do I find Mr. Hanke?

                    CARL
          He's inside. Just leave it here.
          Ain't in the way.

                    SCOTTY
          Thank you.

Scotty heads into the garage.

12   INT. MAPLE GROVE GAS STATION - GARAGE   12

The gas station has two repair bays. Both have cars in them
in some stage of repair. ED HANKE, late 30's and thin, in
dirty gray herringbone coveralls, leans over into one of the
cars engine compartments. Ed is a pragmatic, hard-working,
and self-reliant Midwesterner.

Ed is MUDDLING something to himself as he works. Scotty
stands alongside the car, but Ed is too focused on his work
to notice. A moment passes.

                    SCOTTY
          Excuse me, Mr. Hanke?

Ed is a little startled to see Scotty.

                    ED
          Oh, well, hello there. Sorry, I
          didn't see you.

Ed straightens up and wipes off his hands with a rag.

                    ED (CONT'D)
          I'm Ed Hanke. How can I help you?

He offers his hand to Scotty. Scotty shakes his hand.

                    SCOTTY
          Rick Scott. Sorry to bother you
          sir, but my car just quit on me. I
          was wondering if you could take a
          look?

                                        (CONTINUED)

                    ED
          Well, they do that sometimes. Where's
          it at?

                    SCOTTY
          Just outside.

                    ED
          Why don't we take a look?

Scotty grins and nods. They walk out to the car.

13   EXT. MAPLE GROVE GAS STATION - SCOTTY'S CAR   13

Ed looks over the car.

                    ED
          Nice looking automobile. Pretty
          new, huh?

                    SCOTTY
          Last year.

Ed pops open the hood.

                    ED
          Let's open her up and see what we
          got.

Ed looks over the engine and nods.

                    ED (CONT'D)
          Nice. Go ahead and turn her over.

Scotty gets in and tries to start the engine. It turns over,
but just won't start.

                    ED (CONT'D)
          Well, it seems you got no spark or
          no gas.

                    SCOTTY
          Tank is half full. That means
          carburetor or coil.

                    ED
          That'd be my guess. You a mechanic?

                    SCOTTY
          Kinda, my father taught me all about
          cars.

                    ED
          Best way to learn.
                    (MORE)

                                        (CONTINUED)

                    ED (CONT'D)
          Try to teach Eddie Jr., but he just
          don't seem interested right now.
          Always with the baseball.

                    SCOTTY
          I can understand that. So, do you
          think you can fix it?

                    ED
          I can, but can't get to it today.
          Probably tomorrow sometime. Got two
          ahead of you.
               (pause)
          You're welcome to use the garage and
          my tools if you wanna take a shot at
          it.

Scotty smiles.

                    SCOTTY
          Thank you, sir. That'd be great.

                    ED
          The names, Ed.

                    SCOTTY
          My friends call me "Scotty".

                    ED
          Well Scotty, start whenever you like.
          Carl can help you out.

                    SCOTTY
          Thank you, sir...Ed. Been driving
          all day. If its OK, I think I'll
          check in and start in the morning.

Ed smiles and nods.

Scotty grabs his leather jacket from the front seat and pulls
an old duffel bag from the trunk. Ed notices the jacket and
the duffel bag.

                    ED
          You a service man?

                    SCOTTY
          Navy.

                    ED
          I did '44 and '45 in Europe with the
          Army.

                                             (CONTINUED)

                         SCOTTY
          Carrier in the Pacific in '45.

                         ED
          Rough place. You work with airplanes?

                         SCOTTY
          Something like that. It was all
          rough. Glad you made it back safely,
          Ed.

Ed smiles and shoots Scotty a quick salute. Scotty grins
and ambles toward the motel office.

Scotty hears the RUMBLE of an airplane and looks up to see
an old WWII era J-5A Piper Cub Army observation plane, still
painted Army Olive drab green with Victory stripes, cruise
overhead. He enters the motel office.

14   INT. MAPLE GROVE MOTEL OFFICE   14

The motel office and coffee shop share a separate building
and sit side by side. The side door leads into the office
and the coffee shop entrance is in front.

Scotty enters the office and the screen door closes behind
him with a BA-BUMP. The office is simple and homey with a
counter in the center. A glass-domed cake plate loaded with
muffins sits on one corner of the counter. A few shelves
and hooks with Route 66 souvenirs and maps hang on the walls.

LORRAINE HANKE, mid-30's, with short, dark hair, mid-western
charm and a girl-next-door attractiveness, is waiting behind
the counter with a big smile. Hard work and determination
have made Lorraine wise beyond her years. She is the
foundation of her family, which is the most important thing
in her life.

Scotty sets his jacket on the counter next to him and duffel
bag on the floor.

                         LORRAINE
          Good afternoon, sir.

                         SCOTTY
          Good afternoon. Would you have a
          place for me tonight?

                         LORRAINE
          We sure do. What is the name?

                         SCOTTY
          Rick Scott.

                                        (CONTINUED)

                    LORRAINE
          OK, Mr. Scott. We have cabin 7 all
          ready for you. If you would please
          sign our register.
               (a beat)
          And, help yourself to some fresh
          muffins.

Scotty fills in the register and signs. Lorraine hands Scotty
the key. Scotty grabs a couple of muffins.

                    SCOTTY
          Thank you, ma'am.

                    LORRAINE
          My name's Lorraine and if there is
          anything you need, just let me know.

                    SCOTTY
          Thank you. I will. Please, call me
          Scotty.

He holds out his hand and Lorraine shakes it.

He slips on his jacket and cradles the muffins in one hand.
He picks up his duffel bag with his free hand and exits.

15   EXT. MAPLE GROVE MOTEL OFFICE - DUSK   15

Scotty steps outside. The sun is setting and a soft orange
glow colors the sky.

It is a quiet evening and traffic on Route 66 out front is
light. Some guests sit on the front porch of their cabins,
while others play with their children on the spacious green
that buffers the cabins from the road. A RADIO is softly
playing inside one of the cabins. All against the backdrop
of crickets CHIRPING and cicadas SINGING in the grove.

MOTEL CABINS

Scotty finds his cabin. Each cabin has a ground level porch
that stretches the width of the cabin. The door is centered
between two windows. A bench sits on the left-hand side
right below a window. He unlocks the door and steps inside.

16   INT. CABIN #7   16

Scotty enters and puts the muffins on a small table that
sits in front of the window that overlooks the front porch.

The interior is neat and clean. The main room includes a
couch and a small side table with a radio, on the right side.
A kitchenette is on the left side.

                                        (CONTINUED)

A bathroom mid-way on the left side separates the kitchenette from the two bedrooms located at the back of the cabin.

Scotty tosses his duffel bag into one of the bedrooms. He finds a BASEBALL GAME on the radio, grabs the muffins and stretches out on the couch. He finishes the muffins and within minutes falls sound asleep.

17   INT. CABIN #7 - MORNING - NEXT DAY - TUESDAY, JUNE 30, 1953   17

Scotty awakens still fully dressed and realizes what had happened. He shakes the sleep from his head and stretches.

He shuffles into the bedroom and returns with some clothes from his duffel. Scotty exits into the bathroom.

18   INT. MOTEL COFFEE SHOP - LATER   18

The Coffee/Sandwich shop is more of a small diner than just a Coffee Shop. It is galley-style with a counter on one side with stools, and small booths opposite the counter next to the windows.

Scotty enters and finds Lorraine working behind the counter. He takes a seat at the counter.

                    LORRAINE
          Good morning.

                    SCOTTY
          Good morning, Lorraine. You work in
          the coffee shop, too?

                    LORRAINE
          And, I do the book keeping and most
          of the housekeeping. You see, my
          husband Ed and I own the place.

                    SCOTTY
          You mean Ed Hanke I met last night?

                    LORRAINE
          That's right!

                    SCOTTY
          You two must be pretty busy.

                    LORRAINE
          We bought the motel about three years
          ago. Money's tight so we do most of
          the work ourselves. It's been a
          struggle, but I think we're going to
          make it.

                                        (CONTINUED)

                    SCOTTY
          I hope you do. This is a great place.

                    LORRAINE
          Why, thank you. What can I get for
          you this morning?

                    SCOTTY
          How about some black coffee, and do
          you have any more of those muffins?

                    LORRAINE
          Sure do. My sister bakes them.

Lorraine offers Scotty a selection of muffins from a platter.

                    SCOTTY
          Well, she's one heck of a baker.

Scotty selects three while Lorraine pours him a cup of coffee.
Lorraine is amused by his appetite for the muffins.

                    LORRAINE
          If you don't mind me asking, what
          brings you to Maple Grove?

                    SCOTTY
          Well, my company transferred me to a
          new office in Los Angeles, so, I
          decided to drive. This is my
          vacation.

                    LORRAINE
          Oh my, what do you do?

                    SCOTTY
          We're involved in the new electronics
          industry.

                    LORRAINE
          Salesman?

Scotty hesitates for a moment and takes a sip of his coffee.

                    SCOTTY
          Something like that.

                    LORRAINE
          Well, welcome to Maple Grove.

Eight year-old EDDIE HANKE enters the Coffee Shop and
interrupts.

                                        (CONTINUED)

                    EDDIE
          Hey mom, have you seen my baseball
          mitt?

                    LORRAINE
               (sternly)
          Edward! I'm talking with Mr. Scott.
          Please don't be rude.

Eddie lowers his head and mumbles.

                    EDDIE
          Sorry.

                    LORRAINE
               (to Scotty)
          This is our son, Eddie Jr. Eddie,
          this is Mr. Scott.

Eddie holds out his hand.

                    EDDIE
          Nice to meet you, Mr. Scott.

Scotty shakes his hand.

                    SCOTTY
          Nice to meet you. You like baseball?

                    EDDIE
          Sure do!

                    LORRAINE
          He never stops. Baseball, baseball,
          baseball.

                    SCOTTY
          Who's your team?

                    EDDIE
          St. Louis!

                    SCOTTY
          Oooh..I'm a Yankee fan!

                    EDDIE
          We're gonna take'em this year!

                    SCOTTY
          C'mon! Top of their division. Won
          the pennant and the series last year.

                    EDDIE
          Not this year!

                                        (CONTINUED)

Scotty rummages through his pockets and pulls out some
baseball cards.

                    SCOTTY
          Got these the other day. Not my
          team. You want them?

Eddie looks at his mother for permission. She smirks and
nods her approval.

                    EDDIE
          Sure, thanks!

Scotty hands Eddie the cards. Eddie shuffles through them.
One in particular excites him.

                    EDDIE (CONT'D)
          Wow, Stan the Man! Mom, Stan the
          Man. This is swell. Thanks, Mr.
          Scott!

                    LORRAINE
          Yes, yes, Stan the Man. Now scoot!
          Go find your mitt and let Mr. Scott
          eat his breakfast.

Eddie grabs Scotty's hand and shakes it again.

                    EDDIE
          Thanks, Mr. Scott!

Scotty CHUCKLES and Eddie exits.

                    LORRAINE
          That was very kind of you. I think
          you've made a new friend.

                    SCOTTY
          I was just like that when I was a
          kid. And, you can never have enough
          friends.
               (a beat)
          Well, Ed offered to let me use the
          garage to work on my car. I'd better
          get going.

Scotty places his payment on the counter and gets up.

                    SCOTTY (CONT'D)
          Great muffins!

                    LORRAINE
          I'll tell my sister.

Scotty nods and exits.

19   INT. MAPLE GROVE GAS STATION - GARAGE - MOMENTS LATER   19

Scotty enters. Ed is already working when Scotty arrives.

                         ED
              Mornin'.

                      SCOTTY
              Good morning, Ed.

                         ED
              There's coveralls on the bench if
              you wanna use 'em.

Scotty goes to the work bench and grabs the coveralls

                      SCOTTY
              Thanks.

Scotty slips into the coveralls.

                   SCOTTY (CONT'D)
              Lorraine told me about your little
              venture here.

                         ED
              Couldn't do it without her.

                      SCOTTY
              She seems like a great gal.

Scotty grabs a screwdriver and some pliers from the work
bench.

                         ED
              She's one of a kind!
                 (a beat)
              Eddie was pretty excited about the
              baseball cards. Means a lot to an
              eight-year old boy...and his father.

Scotty acknowledges Ed with a nod.

                      SCOTTY
              You have a nice family, Ed.

20   EXT. MAPLE GROVE GAS STATION   20

Scotty comes out of the garage and walks to his car. He
pops the hood. Eddie joins him.

                      EDDIE
              Whatcha doin' Mr. Scott?

                                              (CONTINUED)

                    SCOTTY
          Gonna find out why this darn thing
          won't run.

Scotty leans over the driver side fender and into the engine
compartment. Eddie watches from in front.

Scotty pulls a spark plug wire and inserts the tip of the
screwdriver into the end of the wire.

                    SCOTTY (CONT'D)
               (to Eddie)
          Can you turn the key for me?

                    EDDIE
          Sure!

Eddie runs over and pulls open the driver side door. He
climbs onto the front seat.

                    SCOTTY
          Turn it when I tell you.

Eddie nods.

                    SCOTTY (CONT'D)
          OK. Go ahead.

The engine turns over and over with a WHIRRR, but will not
start.

                    SCOTTY (CONT'D)
          OK. OK.

Eddie rejoins Scotty.

                    SCOTTY (CONT'D)
          Looks like I have a bad coil.

                    EDDIE
          How can you tell?

                    SCOTTY
          Well, I put the tip of the screwdriver
          into the spark plug wire and held it
          next to a piece of bare metal. I
          should see a spark when you turn it
          over.

                    EDDIE
          No spark?

                    SCOTTY
          No spark.

                                        (CONTINUED)

Ed comes out of the garage wiping his hands on a rag.

                    ED
          Got yourself a helper, did ya?

                    EDDIE
          No spark. We got a bad coil!

Scotty confirms Eddie's diagnosis with a nod. Ed grins at
Eddie and shakes his head.

                    ED
          I don't have one for that car, but I
          can get it. Take a day or so, sorry.

                    SCOTTY
          I'm in no big hurry.

                    ED
          OK, I'll take care of it.

                    SCOTTY
          Say Ed, can I help out in the garage?
          I don't get to work on cars much
          anymore.

                    ED
          You're a guest here, but suit
          yourself. I can use all the help I
          can get.

Ed exits into the garage. Scotty closes the hood on his car
and follows Ed with Eddie in tow.

21   EXT. VIVIAN'S BAKE SHOP   21

The shop is open and some cars are parked out front.

22   INT. VIVIAN'S BAKE SHOP   22

Vivian has her hair tied up in a ponytail as she busily stocks
the display cases with freshly baked items.

BRYCE TOWNSEND enters with newspaper in hand. Bryce is the
local banker; an Ivy league educated, hometown boy who
believes he and Vivian are meant to be.

                    BRYCE
          Oooh, it smells good in here! How's
          my girl?

Vivian is miffed.

                    VIVIAN
          I've warned you about that!

                              (CONTINUED)

Bryce ignores her and sits at a cafe table. Vivian pours a
cup of coffee, pulls a doughnut from a display case and serves
them to Bryce.

                    VIVIAN (CONT'D)
          Bryce, you're a banker. Think I
          could get a loan for my franchise
          idea?

Vivian goes back about her work.

                    BRYCE
          Franchise! That's a big word. Why
          would anyone want to pay to use your
          name on their business?

                    VIVIAN
          Because my stuff is good and customers
          would know they were always getting
          a quality product!

                    BRYCE
          A fad. It's not going to last.
          Besides, it's not a game a woman
          should be playing.

Vivian is indignant.

                    VIVIAN
          Oh, so it's a man's "game"!?

Bryce retreats.

                    BRYCE
          I'm sorry. But, I don't make the
          rules. You're doing fine right here.

Vivian scowls at him and shakes her head.

                    VIVIAN
          Not if I keep giving away free coffee
          and doughnuts!

                    BRYCE
          OK. OK. I'll look into it for you.

Vivian pours herself a cup of coffee and joins him. Bryce
does not acknowledge her and reads his newspaper as he eats.

23   EXT. MAPLE GROVE GAS STATION - GARAGE - LATE AFTERNOON   23

A THUNDERSTORM sweeps across the plains in the distance.
Scotty stands in a garage doorway watching. Ed joins him.

                                              (CONTINUED)

                         SCOTTY
          Thunderstorms have always fascinated
          me.

                         ED
          They're beautiful at a distance.
          But that one's comin' our way.
               (a beat)
          Maybe it'll be good for business.
          Folks don't like drivin' in a storm.

                         SCOTTY
          Business that bad?

                         ED
          Could be better.

                         SCOTTY
          OK Ed, I'm bushed. It's quittin'
          time.

                         ED
          Not for me.

Scotty slips off his coveralls.

                         SCOTTY
          You work a long day.

                         ED
          It'll pay off in the end.

Scotty tosses the coveralls on the workbench.

                         SCOTTY
          I think I'll head over to the coffee
          shop and grab some dinner.

Scotty heads out.

                         ED
          Try the meatloaf sandwich. You won't
          be disappointed.

Scotty turns and waves as he continues on his way.

                         ED (CONT'D)
          And tell Lorraine I'll be up in about
          an hour.

Scotty waves again without turning.

24   INT. CABIN #7 - MOMENTS LATER   24

Scotty enters. He picks up the phone and DIALS the OPERATOR.

                                        (CONTINUED)

                    OPERATOR (V.O.)
          Operator.

                    SCOTTY
          I'd like to make a collect call to
          Manhattan 5, 0-1-8-7. This is Mr.
          Scott.

                    OPERATOR (V.O.)
          Surely.

The phone RINGS on the other end. Tommy answers it.

                    TOMMY (V.O.)
          Scott enterprises, Tom Boyd.

                    OPERATOR (V.O.)
          Collect call from Mr. Scott.

                    TOMMY (V.O.)
          Of course, put him through.

                    OPERATOR (V.O.)
          Go ahead.

                    SCOTTY
          I knew you'd still be in the office.

                    TOMMY (V.O.)
          Scotty! How's L.A.?

                    SCOTTY
          Almost there. A little car trouble.
          No big deal.

                    TOMMY (V.O.)
          What!

                    SCOTTY
          I want you to do something for me.
          I want you to put an ad in the Times
          Sunday travel section.

                    TOMMY (V.O.)
          What does this have to do with your
          car?

                    SCOTTY
          Just do it. It needs to read, "Maple
          Grove Motor Court, the place to stay
          on Route 66. Private cabins,
          luncheonette and pool. Automotive
          services available. Maple Grove,
          Illinois. Jackson 9, 5-7-3-7".
                    (MORE)

                                        (CONTINUED)

                    SCOTTY (CONT'D)
          Get marketing to help you punch it
          up if you need to.

                    TOMMY (V.O.)
          Hold on. Jackson 9, 5-7-3-7.
               (a beat)
          Got it. Do you wanna tell me what's
          going on?

                    SCOTTY
          Just helping out an old service buddy.
          Make sure that gets in for Sunday.

                    TOMMY (V.O.)
          Will do. Can I reach you at this
          place if I need...

                    SCOTTY
          --OK, gotta go if I'm going to get
          to L.A. on time.

     Scotty hangs up with a CLICK.

25   INT. MOTEL COFFEE SHOP - MOMENTS LATER   25

     Scotty enters and sits at the counter. There are a few other
     CUSTOMERS in the shop. Lorraine brings Scotty a cup of
     coffee.

                    LORRAINE
          Ed con you into working in the garage?

     Scotty sips his coffee.

                    SCOTTY
          Nope, I volunteered. Oh, and he
          said he'd be up in about an hour.

     Lorraine places some tableware and a napkin on the counter.

                    LORRAINE
          Mm-hmm. What can I get for you?

                    SCOTTY
          Ed said I should try the meatloaf
          sandwich.

                    LORRAINE
          Always a favorite.

                    SCOTTY
          And can I get another one of those
          muffins?

                                        (CONTINUED)

Lorraine smiles and nods.

                         LORRAINE
               They're in the glass dish on the
               counter. Take what you want.

Lorraine exits into the kitchen. Scotty gets up and grabs
two muffins and sits back down.

Lorraine returns and pours more coffee in his cup. Scotty
breaks into a muffin.

                         LORRAINE (CONT'D)
               What're you doing working in the
               garage? I thought you were on
               vacation?

                         SCOTTY
               I am, but I enjoy it. Some of my
               happiest memories are of working on
               my cars on lazy summer afternoons.

                         LORRAINE
               Baseball and cars. Little boys never
               do grow up.

Scotty grins.

                         SCOTTY
               Not if we don't have to.

Lorraine exits and returns with his meatloaf sandwich. She
goes to wait on some other customers while Scotty eats.

26   INT. CABIN #7 - MORNING - NEXT DAY - WEDNESDAY, JULY 1, 1953   26

Scotty pulls a baseball, mitt, and bat out of his duffel
bag, and exits out the door.

27   EXT. MAPLE GROVE MOTEL - OPEN FIELD - MOMENTS LATER   27

Eddie tosses a ball to himself in a field alongside the coffee
shop. Scotty joins him.

                         EDDIE
               Mornin' Mr. Scott.

                         SCOTTY
               Edward.

Scotty drops the bat and ball on the ground.

                         EDDIE
               Am I in trouble? 'Cause my mom calls
               me Edward when I'm in trouble.

                                        (CONTINUED)

                    SCOTTY
          No, No. Sorry Eddie.

                    EDDIE
          Whatcha got?

                    SCOTTY
          My mitt and a bat. I thought we
          could play hit the bat.

Eddie picks up the bat and starts swinging it.

                    SCOTTY (CONT'D)
          OK slugger, easy. You can have first
          ups.

                    EDDIE
          Swell.

Eddie grabs a ball and heads off into the field and faces
Scotty.

                    SCOTTY
          OK batter. Let's see what you got!

Eddie tosses the ball into the air, swings at it and misses.

                    SCOTTY (CONT'D)
          Aw, no batter, no batter.

Eddie tosses and swings again, but this time connects with a
ground ball to Scotty. Scotty scoops it up.

Eddie lays the bat on the ground and Scotty rolls the ball
trying to "hit the bat". He misses, but it's obvious it was
intentional.

COFFEE SHOP PARKING AREA

Vivian arrives in her 1948 Ford Coupe and parks in front of
the shop. She gets out and removes a box of baked goods
from the passenger side. Eddie and Scotty are playing ball
in the background.

BACK TO SCENE

Scotty notices Vivian as he picks up Eddie's latest hit. He
watches her as she enters the coffee shop.

                    EDDIE
          Hey, Mr. Scott, let's go!

Scotty is distracted by Vivian for a moment.

                                        (CONTINUED)

                    SCOTTY
          Hey Eddie, who's that lady?

                    EDDIE
          That ain't no lady, that's my aunt
          Vivian.

                    SCOTTY
          <u>Aunt</u> Vivian? Your mom's sister?

                    EDDIE
          Yeah. She makes all the cakes and
          stuff.

Scotty's expression reveals he is intrigued. He tosses the
ball back to Eddie.

                    SCOTTY
          Is that the best you got? C'mon!

Eddie screws up his face in determination, tosses the ball
and swings with all his might.

WHACK. Eddie connects. The ball soars over Scotty's head
and lands squarely in the windshield of Vivian's car with a
dull THUMP.

Eddie drops the bat and runs off.

                    SCOTTY (CONT'D)
          Hey! Where you going?

Mitt in hand, Scotty walks over to survey the damage.

28   EXT. COFFEE SHOP PARKING AREA - VIVIAN'S CAR   28

Scotty arrives on the scene just as Lorraine and Vivian come
out of the coffee shop. They both see the damage at the
same time and Scotty standing alongside the car with mitt in
hand.

Vivian says nothing, but presses her hands to her face in
disbelief.

                    LORRAINE
              (shouts)
          Edward!

Lorraine and Vivian join Scotty next to the car. Vivian
pokes at the ball stuck in her windshield. Lorraine glares
at Scotty awaiting an explanation.

                    SCOTTY
          Well...

                                        (CONTINUED)

                    VIVIAN
          --My windshield!

                    SCOTTY
          Well...

Vivian turns her attention to Scotty, her lips taut and her
eyes ablaze.

                    VIVIAN
          --You shouldn't be playing ball so
          close to the parking lot. And aren't
          you a little old for this?

                    SCOTTY
          Well...I was playing with Eddie and...

Eddie is nowhere to be seen.

                    VIVIAN
          --Who are you?

                    LORRAINE
          Vivian, this is Mr. Scott. He's one
          of our guests here. Scotty, this is
          my sister, Vivian Donnelly. She
          does all the baking for the shop.

Scotty is both enchanted and a little apprehensive at what
might happen next. He holds out his hand.

                    SCOTTY
          Nice to meet you. I told Lorraine
          yours are the best muffins I've ever
          had. I said that, right Lorraine.

Lorraine just nods. She is a bit amused at Scotty's
predicament.

Vivian just scowls at Scotty, her blue eyes fixed upon him,
but then her expression softens.

                    SCOTTY (CONT'D)
          I'll fix it. No problem. Right
          away if Ed has the glass.

                    LORRAINE
          You'll both fix it!
               (shouts again)
          Edward!

Eddie peeks out from the corner of the shop and then slowly
ambles over to Scotty's side.

(CONTINUED)

                    SCOTTY
          Yes, ma'am. Right away.

                    EDDIE
          Yes, ma'am. Hi Aunt Vivian.

Vivian shakes her head, but finds it difficult to stay angry
with Eddie. She smirks and rubs the top of his head. Vivian
hands her keys to Scotty.

                    SCOTTY
          You can use my car...no, wait I still
          have to fix that.

                    VIVIAN
          You seem to have problems with
          automobiles, Mr. Scott

Scotty flashes a sheepish grin.

                    SCOTTY
          You have not caught me at my best.

                    VIVIAN
          I hope not.

                    LORRAINE
          Viv, you can use our car.

Lorraine grins at Scotty as she and Vivian exit to find the
Hanke's car.

                    EDDIE
          I like Aunt Vivian. She's really
          nice.

Scotty nods.

29   EXT. MAPLE GROVE GAS STATION - GARAGE - MOMENTS LATER   29

Scotty and Eddie roll up to the front of the garage in
Vivian's car. The baseball is still stuck in the windshield.
Ed is standing there with Carl. Scotty and Eddie get out of
the car.

                    ED
          That Vivian's car?

                    SCOTTY
          Un huh.

                    ED
               (with a broad grin)
          You met Vivian?

                              (CONTINUED)

                    SCOTTY
          Un huh. You have the glass?

                    ED
          It's you're lucky day! But bad news
          is coil won't be in till tomorrow.

                    SCOTTY
          Well, I'm gonna be busy today.

                    ED
          Un huh.

30   EXT. MOTEL COFFEE SHOP   30

     Lorraine and Vivian stand alongside the Hanke's car - a 1948
     Ford "Woody" Station Wagon.

                    LORRAINE
          He's really very nice and polite.

                    VIVIAN
          Lorraine, how long have you known
          him?

                    LORRAINE
          Only a couple days, but I can tell
          things like that.

     Vivian is skeptical and shakes her head.

                    LORRAINE (CONT'D)
          Helped Ed in the garage all day
          yesterday.

                    VIVIAN
          Why?

                    LORRAINE
          He's waiting for a part for his car,
          and he likes to work on cars. Ed
          says he was in the Navy.

     Vivian shakes her head again.

                    VIVIAN
          Well, mine better be fixed by the
          end of the day.

     Vivian gets into the car.

                    LORRAINE
          It will be.

                                        (CONTINUED)

                    VIVIAN
          You seem pretty sure about that.

Lorraine smiles and nods. Vivian pauses for a moment as she
prepares to deliver a difficult message.

                    VIVIAN (CONT'D)
          Lorraine. I think I might move to
          St. Louis to work on my franchise
          business.

Lorraine's expression reflects her dismay.

                    LORRAINE
          You're family is here.

Lorraine's expression changes as if she knows something Vivian
does not.

                    LORRAINE (CONT'D)
          Your future is here. I can tell
          things like that.

Vivian smiles but she is unconvinced.

                    LORRAINE (CONT'D)
          What's passed is passed.

                    VIVIAN
          You have Ed and Eddie. I have only
          myself to rely on. We'll talk later.

Vivian waves and drives off.

31   EXT. MAPLE GROVE GAS STATION - GARAGE - AFTERNOON   31

Scotty cleans off the windshield he just installed in Vivian's
car while Eddie watches. Ed steps out of the garage to see
the finished product. Carl joins him.

                    SCOTTY
          Perfect. I think she'll be happy.

Ed looks over Scotty's work.

                    ED
          Pretty good.
              (a beat)
          That Vivian's quite a package. But
          don't you dare tell Lorraine I said
          so!

Scotty grins and agrees with a nod.

                                        (CONTINUED)

                    EDDIE
          What's a "package"?

Vivian appears from around the corner. It is unclear if she
heard the conversation.

                    VIVIAN
               (playfully)
          Gentlemen, shouldn't you be working
          instead of standing around?

Scotty snaps to attention.

                    SCOTTY
          It's all set, Miss Donnelly.

He hands her the keys. Vivian examines Scotty's work.

                    VIVIAN
          Very nice. Thank you.

Scotty opens the door for her and she gets in. Scotty just
smiles and nods. He closes the door and watches as she drives
off. Ed notices Scotty's goofy grin.

                    ED
          Oh boy, I've seen that look before.

Scotty grins sheepishly.

                    ED (CONT'D)
          She's a lot like her sister, and
          they don't come no better. But that
          one, she's a firecracker!

                    SCOTTY
          Yeah, well I'm a combat veteran!

                    ED
          Un huh.

He CHUCKLES at Scotty's naivete and exits inside the garage.

                    ED (O.S.) (CONT'D)
          Carl, help me with this tire rack.

Carl hustles inside.

                    SCOTTY
               (to Eddie)
          Well, what do you wanna do now?

There is a loud CRASH from inside the garage.

                                             (CONTINUED)

                         CARL
                      (shouting)
                  Mr. Scott, Mr. Scott!

32   INT. MAPLE GROVE GAS STATION - GARAGE   32

Scotty and Eddie rush inside to find tires strewn about and
Ed lying under the tire rack.

33   INT. MOTEL COFFEE SHOP - LATER   33

Scotty sits with Lorraine and Eddie.

                        LORRAINE
               He's gonna be fine. But he has to
               stay off his feet for a few days.

Lorraine's apprehension shows on her face.

                     LORRAINE (CONT'D)
               How am I going to get all his work
               done?

Eddie wraps his arms around her. Scotty takes her hand and
reassures her.

                        SCOTTY
               It's gonna be OK.

She nods, but is still distraught.

                     SCOTTY (CONT'D)
               You know the part for my car isn't
               in yet, so I'm gonna have to stick
               around for a few days. I'm no Ed,
               but maybe I can help out if that's
               OK?

Tears roll down her cheeks and she smiles. No words are
necessary.

34   EXT. TASTEE FREEZ ICE CREAM STAND - EVENING   34

Scotty drives the Hanke's car as he, Lorraine, and Eddie
arrive at the new Tastee Freez ice cream stand and get out
of the car.

Eddie runs runs ahead of them.

                        LORRAINE
               Remind me to get Ed his ice cream.

Scotty nods. Just then he notices Vivian and Bryce sitting
together at a picnic table out front. Lorraine notices the
disappointment on Scotty's face.

                                              (CONTINUED)

                    LORRAINE (CONT'D)
          You know Scotty, not everything is
          as it appears.

                    SCOTTY
          Yes, ma'am.

Vivian sees them and rushes over. She embraces Lorraine.

                    VIVIAN
          Is Ed OK?

                    LORRAINE
          He's going to be fine. Some old
          tires fell on him.

                    VIVIAN
          If there's anything you need, just
          let me know.

Lorraine smiles and nods.

                    LORRAINE
          Scotty's going to help out until the
          part for his car comes in.

Vivian smiles at him.

                    SCOTTY
          Good evening Miss Donnelly.

                    VIVIAN
          Good evening Mr. Scott.

Bryce joins them.

                    VIVIAN (CONT'D)
              (playfully)
          Maybe you boys should stay away from
          automobiles for a while.

Scotty smirks.

                    VIVIAN (CONT'D)
          Mr. Scott, this is Bryce Townsend.

Scotty stares him straight in the eye and shakes his hand.

                    SCOTTY
          Nice to meet you, sir.

                    BRYCE
          Likewise.

                                        (CONTINUED)

                    EDDIE
          C'mon mom!

Lorraine catches up with Eddie.

                    SCOTTY
               (to Vivian)
          Nice to see you again.

Bryce ignores Scotty and turns to leave. Vivian touches
Scotty gently on the arm.

                    VIVIAN
          Thank you.

                    SCOTTY
          I'm the winner here.

Vivian is a little puzzled by the response, but nods politely
and follows Bryce.

35   EXT. MAPLE GROVE GAS STATION - MORNING - NEXT DAY -   35
     THURSDAY, JULY 2, 1953

Scotty arrives, coffee cup in hand, and enters.

36   INT. MOTEL COFFEE SHOP   36

A DELIVERY MAN enters with a small box.

                    LORRAINE
          Can I help you?

                    DELIVERY MAN
          I have an auto part here for Maple
          Grove.

                    LORRAINE
          Oh, that needs to go to the filling
          station just around the corner.

                    DELIVERY MAN
          Yes, ma'am.

He exits.

37   INT. MAPLE GROVE GAS STATION - GARAGE   37

Scotty places his coffee cup on the workbench and slips on
some coveralls. Carl enters.

                    CARL
          Mornin' Mr. Scott.

                              (CONTINUED)

                    SCOTTY
          Good morning, Carl. We'll get along
          better if you just call me Scotty.

                    CARL
          Yes sir, Mr. Scotty.

Scotty CHUCKLES and shakes his head. Delivery man enters
and sees Scotty.

                    DELIVERY MAN
          Hey, I got a part here for somebody.

                    SCOTTY
          I'll take it.

Scotty signs the receipt and the Delivery man exits.

Scotty opens the box and finds the coil for his car. He
hides it behind a tool box just as he hears the DING DING of
the service call bell.

MONTAGE

-- Scotty works on cars in the garage.

-- Helps repair a farm tractor.

-- Shows Carl how to do some repairs.

-- Lorraine shows up with sandwiches and muffins.

-- Scotty takes payment for some repairs.

38   INT. MOTEL COFFEE SHOP - EVENING   38

Scotty finishes repairing the sink drain. He washes off his
hands and slumps down in one of the booths, exhausted.

Lorraine brings him his dinner.

                    SCOTTY
          Lorraine, Ed's a better man than I
          am.

                    LORRAINE
          Well, Mr. Rucker was pretty happy
          with his tractor. You saved him a
          lot of time and money.

Scotty CHUCKLES.

                                        (CONTINUED)

                    SCOTTY
          Never worked on a tractor before.
          I'm glad I could help! These are
          good people, Lorraine. They work
          hard for their money.

                    LORRAINE
          Did you get that part for your car?

                    SCOTTY
          Oh, not yet.

Lorraine responds with a puzzled squint, but quickly grows
wise to Scotty's ruse. She smiles and pats him on the back.

39 INT. MOTEL COFFEE SHOP - MORNING - NEXT DAY - FRIDAY, JULY   39
    3, 1953

Scotty is just finishing his breakfast when MARK CARR a former
shipmate enters with his WIFE and TWO CHILDREN. They slip
into a booth near the door. Mark notices Scotty and stares
at him for a moment. He finally recognizes Scotty and strides
over to him.

                    MARK
          Scott! Lieutenant Scott.

Scotty turns when he hears his name and instantly recognizes
the man. He jumps up from the counter and the two men
embrace.

                    MARK (CONT'D)
          Great to see you Lieutenant.

                    SCOTTY
          It's just "Scotty" now. It's great
          to see you, too! What're you doing
          here?

                    MARK
          On our way out west for a little
          vacation. Gonna spend the night
          here.

                    SCOTTY
          Great place to stay.

                    MARK
          C'mon over and meet my family.

Lorraine watches from the counter as Scotty goes over to the
booth and is introduced to Mark's family.

Momentarily Lorraine follows.

                                        (CONTINUED)

                    LORRAINE
          I hate to interrupt the reunion,
          gentlemen.

                    SCOTTY
          Mark, this is Lorraine Hanke. She's
          tops and she'll take good care of
          you.
               (to Lorraine)
          This is Mark, an old navy buddy and
          his family. Their breakfast is on
          me.

                    MARK
          C'mon Scotty.

                    SCOTTY
          No arguments sailor!

Mark acknowledges the order.

                    MARK
          Sir.

                    SCOTTY
          I'd like to catch up with you before
          you leave. I'm helping out in the
          garage. Stop by if you have some
          time.

                    MARK
          I'd like that.

Scotty smiles at Mark's wife and children.

                    SCOTTY
          Nice to meet all of you. Well, gotta
          get to work. The boss is a tough
          lady.

Lorraine scowls at him playfully. Scotty LAUGHS. He goes
back to the counter, leaves his payment and exits.

                    LORRAINE
          I've only known him for a few days,
          but he seems like a fine man.

                    MARK
          Lieutenant Scott? He's the best.
          If it weren't for him a lotta men
          would've lost their lives. He's a
          real war hero!

Lorraine is taken by surprise. She cocks her head.

                                        (CONTINUED)

                    LORRAINE
          Scotty never mentioned that.

                    MARK
          Not surprised. That's our Scotty.
          He rammed his plane into a Kamikaze
          that was bearing down on our ship.
          Risked his life to save a lotta men.
          Earned the Medal of Honor and spent
          three months in a hospital. Now I
          hear he owns a big electronics
          company.

                    LORRAINE
          Is that right?

                    MARK
          I owe that man my life.

                    LORRAINE
          Order whatever you like. It's on
          the house.

                    MARK
          He won't like that!

                    LORRAINE
               (authoritatively)
          Don't you worry. I'll deal with
          Lieutenant Scott!

                    MARK
          Yes, ma'am.

     Lorraine takes their order. She stops at the counter on her
     way to the kitchen and picks up the payment Scotty left.
     She pauses for a moment contemplating the man who left it.

40   INT. MAPLE GROVE GAS STATION - GARAGE - LATER   40

     Scotty works on a car with Eddie observing.

     Lorraine arrives with Scotty's lunch. She places it on the
     work bench.

                    LORRAINE
          Lunchtime! Take a break.
               (a beat)
          Eddie, I want to talk to Mr. Scott.
          Go check on your father.

     Eddie scowls, but doesn't argue.

                                                  (CONTINUED)

```
                    EDDIE
              (to Scotty)
     You must be in trouble or something.

                    LORRAINE
              (to Eddie)
     Go!

Eddie exits.  Scotty washes his hands in a nearby sink and
dries them with a rag.

                    SCOTTY
     Anything wrong?

There is a seriousness in Lorraine's tone.

                    LORRAINE
     I need to speak with you, Lieutenant
     Scott!

Scotty takes a deep breath and nods.

                    SCOTTY
     How much did Mark give away?

                    LORRAINE
     Corporate executive?  War hero!

Scotty sits on a stool.

                    LORRAINE (CONT'D)
     What else are you hiding?

                    SCOTTY
     OK.  I'm an engineer, graduated from
     MIT.  While I was in the hospital I
     met a man who helped me create Scott
     Enterprises.  We deal in all types
     of electronics.

                    LORRAINE
     Why wouldn't you tell me?  I thought
     we were friends.

Scotty looks into Lorraine's eyes.  He sees disappointment.

                    SCOTTY
     Please forgive me.  And, I'm no war
     hero.  I did what I had to do.  Just
     like Ed and Mark and all the others.
     And the business part, that's just a
     role I play.  That's not the real
     me.

Lorraine listens without responding.

                                        (CONTINUED)
```

                    SCOTTY (CONT'D)
          I went to war and when I came back,
          everything had changed. People
          treated me differently. Yes, I became
          successful, but when my father, and
          then my mother passed away, it seemed
          like the best part of my life went
          with them. Now that's, the whole
          story.

                    LORRAINE
          The baseball, the cars, the little
          boy hiding inside.

There is emotion in Scotty's eyes.

                    SCOTTY
          I just wanted to be "Scotty" again.
          Pretty pathetic, huh?

Lorraine smiles and takes his hands.

                    LORRAINE
          No. It's all those moments from our
          lives that makes us who we are.
          But, you can't run away from who you
          are now. Things happen for a reason.
          Would you be here today if not for
          Scott Enterprises?
               (a beat)
          I like the Scotty I met a few days
          ago. And, it makes no difference
          war hero or executive.

                    SCOTTY
          Will you keep my secret?

Lorraine thinks for a minute.

                    LORRAINE
          Let me ask you something, and be
          honest! When you look at my sister,
          what do you see?

Scotty is a little puzzled by the question, but responds
thoughtfully.

                    SCOTTY
          A smart, self-assured young woman
          with sparkling blue eyes and a smile
          that lights up all outdoors.

Lorraine smiles.

                                        (CONTINUED)

                    LORRAINE
          Why don't you tell her that? Most
          men only see a pin-up girl, a trophy
          to hang on their arm. She's much
          more than that. She deserves better.

Scotty cocks his head.

                    SCOTTY
          I didn't make such a great first
          impression.

Lorraine dismisses his concern with a wave of her hand.

                    LORRAINE
          It'll be alright. OK. Now about
          that secret.

Scotty's expression turns apprehensive.

                    LORRAINE (CONT'D)
          Ed was supposed to teach me how to
          drive. With him laid up, I figure
          you can fill in.

Scotty is reluctant and it shows on his face.

                    LORRAINE (CONT'D)
          Is it a deal?

Lorraine holds out her hand. Scotty takes a deep breath and
shakes her hand.

                    LORRAINE (CONT'D)
          Good. And mind helping me get Ed to
          the fireworks tomorrow night?
              (a beat)
          Vivian will be there.

Scotty agrees with a nod.

                    SCOTTY
          With Bryce?

                    LORRAINE
          I don't know. Does he concern you?

Scotty indicates he doesn't with a shake his head. Lorraine
smiles. That's what she wanted to hear. She kisses him on
the cheek and exits. Scotty goes back to work.

41   INT. MOTEL COFFEE SHOP - LATER   41

Scotty finishes up his dinner. Lorraine is working at the
counter.

                                                   (CONTINUED)

Eddie enters and stops to see his mother. She gives him
something. Eddie rushes over to Scotty.

                    EDDIE
          Hey Mr. Scott. Mom gave me some
          money and said maybe you could take
          me to the drug store for some baseball
          cards?

                    SCOTTY
          Can do!

Scotty follows Eddie to the door. He stops for a moment as
he passes Lorraine. He smiles at her and exits.

42   EXT. MAIN STREET (ROUTE 66) MAPLE GROVE - LATER   42

Vivian drives down Main Street and sees Scotty and Eddie
walking down the sidewalk in the direction of the motel.
Eddie is shuffling through some baseball cards and showing
selected ones to Scotty.

Vivian pulls over and stops.

                    VIVIAN
          Would you fellas like a ride?

                    EDDIE
          Hi Aunt Vivian. Sure!

Scotty opens the door and Eddie climbs into the back seat.
Scotty sits in front with Vivian.

43   INT. VIVIAN'S CAR   43

She drives.

                    SCOTTY
          Thank you, Miss Donnelly.

                    VIVIAN
          You're welcome. Where have you two
          been?

Eddie holds up the baseball cards.

                    EDDIE
          Got some baseball cards.

                    VIVIAN
          You did? Get any good ones?

                    EDDIE
          Nah, but Mr. Scott gave me Stan the
          Man the other day.

                                        (CONTINUED)

                    VIVIAN
          Stan Musial! That was pretty nice
          of Mr. Scott.

                    SCOTTY
          You know baseball?

Vivian CHUCKLES at Scotty's surprised reaction.

                    VIVIAN
          I love baseball. Well, not so much
          when one lands in my windshield, but
          Lorraine and I used to play with
          Eddie's grandfather all the time.

                    SCOTTY
          You play?

                    VIVIAN
          I may be a little rusty, but I think
          I can still swing a pretty fair bat.
          Surprised?

                    EDDIE
          She's better'n me, Mr. Scott.

Scotty grins at Vivian.

                    SCOTTY
          Actually, no.

Vivian CHUCKLES.

                    VIVIAN
          Don't get a chance to play much
          anymore. The bakery keeps me pretty
          busy. Five in the morning till 6 at
          night, most days.

They arrive at the motel.

                    SCOTTY
          Long hours, but you're very good at
          what you do.

                    VIVIAN
          Thank you. That's always nice to
          hear.

                    SCOTTY
          Thanks for the ride. Always a
          pleasure see you. Good night.

Vivian smiles.

(CONTINUED)

                    VIVIAN
          Good night.

Scotty exits followed by Eddie.

                    VIVIAN (CONT'D)
               (to Eddie)
          Good night, sweetie.

                    EDDIE
          G'night Aunt Vivian. Thanks for the
          ride.

                    VIVIAN
          You're welcome.

Scotty closes the door. Vivian waves and drives off.

44   INT. MOTEL COFFEE SHOP - MORNING - NEXT DAY - SATURDAY, JULY   44
      4, 1953

Sunshine streams through the windows. Lorraine works behind
the counter. Part-time employee DORIS works in the
background.

Vivian enters carrying a box of baked goods. Lorraine hurries
over to help her.

                    VIVIAN
          Good morning Doris.

Doris waves.

                    VIVIAN (CONT'D)
               (to Lorraine)
          Made some, red, white and blue cup
          cakes.

                    LORRAINE
          They look delicious.
               (a beat)
          Are you going to the fireworks with
          us tonight?

                    VIVIAN
          I'll meet you there. Ed going?

                    LORRAINE
          With Scotty's help.

                    VIVIAN
               (jokingly)
          Are you sure that's a good idea.
          Those two seem like an accident
          waiting to happen.

                                        (CONTINUED)

Lorraine CHUCKLES.

                    LORRAINE
          Is Bryce going?

                    VIVIAN
          I'm sure he'll be there.

Lorraine takes Vivian's hands in hers.

                    LORRAINE
          I'm sorry about the other day. If
          you want to go to St. Louis, you
          should go. But be careful what you
          wish for. Is it worth what you'll
          have to give up?

Vivian is uncertain and can only ponder Lorraine's question.

                    LORRAINE (CONT'D)
          Everyone has a little darkness in
          their life. Don't let it blind you.

                    VIVIAN
          I won't do anything before I talk to
          my big sister.

Vivian hugs Lorraine. She turns to leave and then turns
back.

                    VIVIAN (CONT'D)
          You like Mr. Scott, don't you?

                    LORRAINE
          I do. Ed trusts him with the garage
          and Eddie adores him.

                    VIVIAN
          I just get the feeling there's more
          to him than we know.

                    LORRAINE
               (coyly)
          Well, maybe you should ask him.

                    VIVIAN
          Hmm.

Vivian exits.

45   EXT. OPEN FIELD - DUSK   45

The 4th of July is a town celebration in Maple Grove. There
are food and ice cream vendors; balloons and pinwheels for
sale.

                                        (CONTINUED)

Children run around waving sparklers and the more adventurous
light FIRECRACKERS. Families spread out blankets on the
ground and wait for the evening fireworks.

Scotty helps Ed out of the Hanke's car. Lorraine and Eddie
hop out of the back seat.

Lorraine spreads a blanket on the ground and Scotty helps Ed
hobble over and ease down on the blanket. Lorraine joins
him. Eddie is busy opening a box of sparklers.

Scotty spreads another blanket on the ground alongside them.

Eddie finally wrestles a sparkler out of the box.

                    EDDIE
          Can I light it, mom?

Scotty pulls out a lighter.

                    SCOTTY
          I got it.

After a couple tries the sparkler ignites.

                    LORRAINE
          Be careful. Keep it away from your
          face.

Eddie runs off waving the sparkler in the air.

Scotty sits down on his blanket just as Vivian arrives. He
climbs back to his feet.

                    VIVIAN
          Hi Ed. How are you feeling?

                    ED
          I'm fine, but your sister keeps
          fussin' over me.

                    VIVIAN
          Hi Lorraine.

She kneels and hugs Ed and Lorraine. Scotty sits. Vivian
turns her attention to Scotty.

                    VIVIAN (CONT'D)
          Nice to see you again, Mr. Scott.
          Do you mind if I share your blanket?

                    SCOTTY
          Not at all.

She sits next to Scotty.

                                        (CONTINUED)

                    SCOTTY (CONT'D)
          Nice to see you again, Miss Donnelly.

There is a moment of awkward silence. Lorraine just rolls
her eyes at Scotty.

                    VIVIAN
          It's going to be a beautiful evening.
          I love fireworks.

                    SCOTTY
          Reminds me of when I was a kid. I
          was just like Eddie.

More awkward silence.

                    VIVIAN
          So, tell me a little about yourself.

                    SCOTTY
          Not much to tell. I grew up in a
          small town in Connecticut. No
          brothers or sisters. Went to college
          and joined the Navy in '44. Served
          off the coast of Japan.

Lorraine tries to discretely eavesdrop on the conversation.

                    SCOTTY (CONT'D)
          Got out of the navy and started
          working with an electronics company
          in New York. They transferred me to
          Los Angeles and driving out there
          was sort of my vacation. But, had
          some car trouble and stopped here in
          Maple Grove. And, you know the rest.

                    VIVIAN
          And, you like baseball and cars.

Scotty smiles and nods.

                    SCOTTY
          Oh, there is one secret I haven't
          even told Lorraine.

Lorraine's expression turns to surprise. Vivian leans in
close to Scotty.

                    VIVIAN
               (whispering)
          What's that.

                                        (CONTINUED)

                    SCOTTY
               (whispers)
          My family name is really Scotti, S-c-
          o-t-t-i. My parents changed it when
          they arrived from Italy. Thought
          we'd fit in better.

Vivian CHUCKLES.

                    VIVIAN
               (whispering)
          I won't tell anyone.

A moment passes.

                    SCOTTY
          I want to apologize again for the
          windshield.

                    VIVIAN
          No harm. You did a wonderful job
          fixing it. Thank you.

Another awkward moment.

                    SCOTTY
          So, tell me about Vivian Donnelly.

                    VIVIAN
          Hometown girl. Started my own bake
          shop and I get by.
               (enthusiastically)
          You know, I have this idea for
          starting a bakery franchise. I really
          think it could work!
               (she pauses)
          But, some people think I'm just being
          foolish.

                    SCOTTY
          I meant it when I said those were
          the best muffins I've ever had.

                    VIVIAN
          Thank you.

                    SCOTTY
          But be careful what you wish for.

Vivian is perplexed.

                    VIVIAN
          Lorraine said the same thing.

                                        (CONTINUED)

                    SCOTTY
          She's a smart lady.

                    VIVIAN
          She's very fond of you.

                    SCOTTY
          I've grown very fond of her. Ed is
          a great guy and Eddie is a great
          kid.

Vivian studies him for a moment.

                    VIVIAN
          You miss that small town, don't you?

Scotty is surprised by her intuition. He cocks his head and
CHUCKLES.

                    SCOTTY
          You're quite perceptive.

Vivian smiles a sly smile.

                    VIVIAN
          I guess that's just part of the
          package.

Scotty grins sheepishly.

                    VIVIAN (CONT'D)
          I think seeing as my sister has
          practically adopted you, you should
          call me Vivian.

                    SCOTTY
          If you call me Scotty.

Vivian nods. For a moment she gazes into Scotty's eyes.
There's a connection. A moment passes. Scotty takes a
chance.

                    SCOTTY (CONT'D)
          About that comment. We didn't mean
          any disrespect. I apologize.

                    VIVIAN
          It's OK. I've heard it all before.

                    SCOTTY
          No, you deserve better. For the
          record, I told your sister I thought
          you were a smart, self-assured young
          woman...
                    (MORE)

                                        (CONTINUED)

                    SCOTTY (CONT'D)
               (Scotty is caught up
                in her gaze and
                whispers)
          ...with sparkling blue eyes and a
          smile that lights up all outdoors.

Vivian is enchanted.

                    SCOTTY (CONT'D)
          Oooh, that last part. Did I say
          that out loud? I'm sorry.

Vivian cocks her head and takes Scotty's hand. Lorraine is
smiling.

                    VIVIAN
          Thank you.

Just then Bryce arrives.

                    BRYCE
          There's my girl.

Vivian is startled and quickly releases Scotty's hand.

                    VIVIAN
          Oh Bryce. I warned you about that.
               (a beat)
          Would you like to join us.

Bryce and Scotty's expressions show neither is thrilled with
her invitation, but Bryce squeezes in between Lorraine and
Vivian to Lorraine's displeasure.

FIREWORKS illuminate the night sky.

46   INT. MOTEL COFFEE SHOP - MORNING - NEXT DAY - SUNDAY, JULY   46
     5, 1953

Scotty enters and notices a poster on the counter.

INSERT POSTER

which reads "USO NIGHT at the VFW, July 8, 1953 7:30 PM,
Maple Grove VFW POST #2234"

BACK TO SCENE

                    SCOTTY
               (referring to the
                poster)
          What this?

Scotty searches around for the muffins.

                                             (CONTINUED)

                    LORRAINE
          Every year around the fourth the VFW
          has it's USO night. All the hostesses
          dress up as '40s USO girls and the
          men wear their old uniforms.

                    SCOTTY
          No muffins?

                    LORRAINE
          Not yet.

Lorraine serves Scotty a cup of coffee.

                    SCOTTY
          I can wait. So, what happens on USO
          night?

                    LORRAINE
          We have a spaghetti dinner and
          deserts. There's music and dancing,
          and a lot of old war stories.

                    SCOTTY
          Sounds like fun.

                    LORRAINE
          You're welcome to join us if you're
          still here. I'll be one of the USO
          girls. And, Vivian will be joining
          us this year. She's donating all
          the baked goods.

                    SCOTTY
          No telling when that darn part will
          get here. Save me a dance?

Lorraine smiles playfully. The telephone RINGS.

                    LORRAINE
          Of course, sailor.

Lorraine answers the phone.

                    LORRAINE (CONT'D)
          Hello?
               (pause)
          Hi sweetheart.
               (pause)
          OK, I'll send someone over.
               (pause)
          OK. Talk to you later.

Lorraine hangs up the phone.

                                        (CONTINUED)

                    LORRAINE (CONT'D)
          That was Vivian. Sunday mornings
          are her busy time. Do you mind taking
          Eddie with you over there to pick up
          our baked goods?

Scotty grins.

                    SCOTTY
          Will do.

Scotty is on his way before Lorraine can respond.

47   EXT. VIVIAN'S BAKE SHOP   47

Scotty parks out front. He and Eddie climb out of the car.

48   INT. VIVIAN'S BAKE SHOP   48

Scotty and Eddie enter. The shop is busy. Clarice helps
Vivian wait on customers. Bryce is sitting at a table having
his usual doughnut and coffee, and reading a newspaper.

There is a USO Night poster on her counter as well.

                    BRYCE
          Good morning, Mr. Scott.

                    SCOTTY
          Good morning, Mr. Townsend.

Vivian is behind the counter, but notices Scotty and Eddie
enter.

                    VIVIAN
          Good morning, Gentlemen. I'm still
          putting everything together. Just
          have a seat for a minute.

Scotty and Eddie sit at a small table alongside Bryce. Eddie
fidgets. Vivian comes over with a muffin for Scotty and a
doughnut for Eddie. She places them on the table.

                    VIVIAN (CONT'D)
               (to Eddie)
          Here sweetie.

Eddie and Scotty respond simultaneously.

                    EDDIE AND SCOTTY
          Thank you.

Scotty realizes his faux pas and grins sheepishly. Vivian
just smiles, pats him on the back and rushes off again.
They eat in silence.

                                        (CONTINUED)

Moments later as the bakery quiets down Vivian returns with
a box. Scotty rises to help her. He takes the box from
Vivian and places it on the table.

                    SCOTTY
          Can you sit for a minute?

He pulls out a chair and she sits next to Scotty.

                    VIVIAN
          Thank you. Been on my feet all
          morning. Lorraine can call me if
          she needs anything else.

Scotty refers to the USO poster.

                    SCOTTY
          I hear you'll be doing all the baking
          for the USO night. I'm sure the
          vets will appreciate that.

Bryce takes a break from his newspaper.

                    BRYCE
          Dressing up too! Pretty proud of
          Vivian putting the past behind her.

Vivian's expression turns to exasperation.

                    VIVIAN
               (sharply)
          Bryce!

It's clear this is something Vivian does not want to discuss.
Scotty notices, but says nothing. Bryce retreats.

                    BRYCE
          I understand you were a sailor.
          Will you be joining us?

Vivian is a little flushed. Scotty relieves the tension
when he glances at her and smiles.

                    SCOTTY
          I wouldn't miss it.

                    BRYCE
          I was a master sergeant in logistical
          command. France '45.

                    SCOTTY
          Carrier in the Pacific.

                    BRYCE
          You work in aviation?

                                        (CONTINUED)

                    SCOTTY
          Something like that.

Scotty stands and picks up the box.

                    SCOTTY (CONT'D)
          Let's go Eddie. Your mom is waiting
          for this.

                    VIVIAN
          Thank you for helping out. Would
          you tell Lorraine I'll see her later?

                    SCOTTY
          You're welcome. I'll let her know.
          Nice to see you again Vivian.

Eddie leads Scotty out of the bakery. Vivian watches them
go.

                    BRYCE
          Seems like a nice enough guy.

Vivian doesn't respond. She is still watching Scotty as he
exits.

                    VIVIAN
          What? Oh, yes. Yes, he does.

Bryce's puzzled expression suggests he is unsure how to take
the whole exchange. He goes back to his breakfast and
newspaper.

49   INT. MOTEL COFFEE SHOP   49

Scotty and Eddie arrive with the box of baked goods and place
it on the counter. Scotty takes a seat at the counter while
Lorraine unpacks the box with Eddie's help.

                    LORRAINE
          Eddie, slow down.

Eddie grabs a doughnut and starts to rush off. Scotty
snatches a muffin.

                    LORRAINE (CONT'D)
               (to Eddie)
          Wait! Take these to your father.

She wraps two doughnuts and hands them to Eddie. He exits.

                    EDDIE
          See ya later Mr. Scott.

                                        (CONTINUED)

                         SCOTTY
                    See ya.

Lorraine pours Scotty a cup of coffee. She starts placing
items in the display case and on the counter.

                         LORRAINE
                    Got a call this morning from New
                    York.

                         SCOTTY
                    Oh yeah? Who do you know in New
                    York?

                         LORRAINE
                    No one. This gentlemen said he saw
                    our ad in the Times travel section.
                    Wanted to make a reservation.

Scotty grins sheepishly.

                         SCOTTY
                    That's good.

                         LORRAINE
                    I didn't place an ad in the Times.

She stares at Scotty. He tries to avoid her stare.

                         SCOTTY
                      (without looking up)
                    Seemed like a good idea at the time.

He looks up. She cocks her head, then shakes her head and
smirks at him.

                         LORRAINE
                    That was very generous, but you didn't
                    have to do it. You owe us nothing!

                         SCOTTY
                    OK. I won't do it again.

Her expression shows she doesn't believe him, but accepts
the answer for the time being.

                         LORRAINE
                    Un huh.

                         SCOTTY
                    Do you think it'll help?

                         LORRAINE
                    I hope so.

                                        (CONTINUED)

                    SCOTTY
          I know its none of my business, but
          are things that bad.

                    LORRAINE
          Not bad, but its getting harder to
          compete. Now all the motels are
          getting the new television sets. We
          just don't have enough in the budget
          yet. Bryce offered to give us a
          loan for the difference, but--

                    SCOTTY
          --How many do you need?

                    LORRAINE
          Well, one for each cabin.

                    SCOTTY
          So that's 10. How much do you have
          in your budget?

                    LORRAINE
          Only about $800.

                    SCOTTY
          You know, I think that's just enough.

She realizes instantly what he is doing.

                    LORRAINE
          Scotty!

                    SCOTTY
          What? My company sells TVs. You
          need TVs. It's a simple business
          deal.

                    LORRAINE
          I know you can't get 10 TV's for
          $800.

                    SCOTTY
               (firmly)
          Excuse me, but that's my business
          and yes, you can.
               (his demeanor softens)
          Please, let me do this.

She shakes her head reluctantly.

                    SCOTTY (CONT'D)
          Lorraine, I have no one to share my
          success with.
                    (MORE)

                                        (CONTINUED)

                    SCOTTY (CONT'D)
          For the last few days you and Ed and
          Eddie have shared your life with me.
          Please. It'll be our secret.

She tearfully accepts with nod. She comes around the counter
and hugs him.

                    SCOTTY (CONT'D)
          Any more muffins?

Lorraine picks up the whole plate and places it in front of
him and goes back to work.

                    SCOTTY (CONT'D)
          What's the deal with Bryce and Vivian?

Scotty picks out his favorite muffins.

                    LORRAINE
          He thinks he's perfect and she's not
          sure. He's nice enough, but I think
          she deserves better.

                    SCOTTY
          She said she had an idea for expanding
          the bake shop.

                    LORRAINE
          She wants to go to St. Louis and try
          some --franchise-- thing.

                    SCOTTY
          That's pretty ambitious.

                    LORRAINE
          That's my sister.

Scotty smiles and nods.

                    SCOTTY
          A real firecracker.

                    LORRAINE
          You've been talking to Ed. Do you
          think she can do it?

                    SCOTTY
          I think she can accomplish anything
          she wants. Not sure it's worth the
          cost.

                    LORRAINE
          Maybe she needs someone to help her
          realize that.

                                        (CONTINUED)

Scotty responds with a smirk signaling to Lorraine she has
made her point. He finishes his coffee and muffins.

>   SCOTTY
>   I'm going down to the garage to see
>   if Carl needs any help.

>   LORRAINE
>   Get your part yet?

>   SCOTTY
>   Going to check on it.

Scotty exits. Lorraine smirks, but doesn't let on she knows.

50   EXT. MAPLE GROVE GAS STATION - AFTERNOON   50

Scotty and Carl sit out front on a lazy, summer Sunday,
afternoon. Suddenly, an excited Eddie appears from around
the corner with his baseball mitt. He runs up to Scotty.

>   EDDIE
>   Hey, Mr. Scott, Aunt Vivian came
>   over with her baseball mitt!

>   SCOTTY
>   What?!

>   EDDIE
>   C'mon, ya gotta see!

Scotty glances at Carl.

>   CARL
>   I'm OK here.

Scotty follows Eddie to the coffee shop.

51   EXT. MOTEL COFFEE SHOP - MOMENTS LATER   51

Vivian's car is parked out front.

52   INT. MOTEL COFFEE SHOP   52

Eddie enters followed by Scotty.

Lorraine is behind the counter. Vivian is sitting at the
counter dressed in baggy blue jeans, a white t-shirt, and
black hi-top sneakers. Her baseball mitt and a ball sit on
the counter. A small canvas bag filled with more baseballs
sits on the floor next to her.

>   SCOTTY
>   What's going on?

(CONTINUED)

Vivian gets up and tosses him the baseball.

> VIVIAN
> Let's see what ya got, sailor. A
> little home run derby?

A broad smile crosses Scotty's face.

> EDDIE
> C'mon Mr. Scott, you can beat 'er!

> VIVIAN
> Eddie, I'm your Aunt! You have to
> cheer for me.

Eddie glances at Vivian and then Lorraine in bewilderment.

> EDDIE
> Do I, mom?

Lorraine nods.

> EDDIE (CONT'D)
> Aw, OK.

> SCOTTY
> OK. I'll take that challenge.

Eddie grabs the bag with the balls. Scotty, Eddie, and
Vivian head out to the field next to the motel. Lorraine
goes back to work.

53   EXT. OPEN FIELD NEXT TO COFFEE SHOP   53

Eddie and Vivian play catch. Scotty returns after retrieving
his mitt and a bat from his cabin.

Scotty gets first "ups" at bat and Eddie plays the outfield.
Vivian takes the bag of balls and pitches to Scotty.

SERIES OF SHOTS

Scotty bats and then Vivian. The object is to hit as many
home runs as possible before getting 3 outs. Scotty does
not do as well as he had hoped.

54   INT. MOTEL COFFEE SHOP - LATER   54

Eddie, Scotty, and Vivian enter.

Eddie shuffles in carrying the bag of balls and looks a little
disappointed. He sets the bag on the floor near the counter.
Scotty wears a sheepish expression. Vivian is smiling.
They all sit but say nothing.

(CONTINUED)

                    LORRAINE
          Well? Who won?

                     EDDIE
          Aunt Vivian, again.

Vivian beams with gratification.

                    LORRAINE
               (to Scotty)
          Maybe I should have warned you.

Scotty smirks.

                    VIVIAN
          OK boys, let's hear it!

Eddie grudgingly walks over and shakes Vivian's hand.

                     EDDIE
          Good job, Aunt Vivian.

She grabs him and gives him a hug.

                    VIVIAN
          Thank you, Eddie.

Vivian looks at Scotty with arched brow waiting for his
concession. He turns and shakes her hand.

                    SCOTTY
               (playfully)
          You're pretty good for a girl.

Vivian LAUGHS.

                    SCOTTY (CONT'D)
          No hug?

Vivian cocks her head and smirks. She hugs Scotty.

                    VIVIAN
          Well, I've gotta go and check on
          Clarice.

She grabs her mitt and rises.

                    VIVIAN (CONT'D)
          See you tomorrow, Lorraine.

                    LORRAINE
          Bye, sweetheart.

Vivian picks up the bag and starts towards the door. Lorraine
nods to Scotty. He gets up and takes the bag from Vivian.

                                             (CONTINUED)

                         SCOTTY
              Let me get that for you.

She smiles and he follows her out the door.

55   EXT. COFFEE SHOP PARKING AREA   55

Vivian and Scotty walk to her car. Vivian opens the door
and tosses her mitt into the back seat. Scotty places the
bag of balls on the floor behind the driver's seat.

Scotty holds the door while Vivian gets in. He closes the
door and leans in the window.

                         SCOTTY
              I want a rematch.

                         VIVIAN
              Anytime.

Scotty lingers. There's something he wants to say.

                         SCOTTY
              Vivian, it's none of my business,
              but Lorraine says you want to move
              to St. Louis and build a business
              empire.

Vivian CHUCKLES.

                         VIVIAN
              Is that what she says!?

Scotty grins.

                         SCOTTY
              Not exactly, but is that what you
              really want?

                         VIVIAN
              Would it be so bad? I don't know
              what kind of future I have here.

                         SCOTTY
              Ed and Lorraine seem to be happy.

                         VIVIAN
              Lorraine has Ed and Eddie.

                         SCOTTY
              Why can't you have the same thing?

There is anguish in her eyes.

                                              (CONTINUED)

                    VIVIAN
          I seem to be the kind of girl men
          like to be around, but don't want to
          keep around.

An expression of disbelief colors Scotty's face.

                    SCOTTY
          What? You don't really believe that,
          do you?

She looks into his eyes.

                    VIVIAN
          I'm not sure what to believe anymore.

                    SCOTTY
          You have to decide what you really
          want, and take a chance. You might
          be surprised.

She pats him gently on the cheek and smiles.

                    VIVIAN
          Thank you for your concern. I'll be
          fine.
               (a beat)
          And, I'll tell my sister you tried.

Scotty backs away and watches her drive off.

56   EXT. VIVIAN'S HOUSE - DUSK   56

A small Craftsman house sits on a back road just outside of
town. Houses are spread far apart here. Vivian's house is
surrounded by a landscape of endless open fields dotted with
groves of trees.

Vivian sits alone on the front porch. In her hands she holds
a time worn envelope. She slips a letter out and slowly
unfolds it. It has the look of a document that has been
read and re-read.

INSERT LETTER

neatly handwritten which reads, "March 3, 1946, Dear Vivian,
There is no easy way to say this. You are a great girl, but
I've met someone here in Japan. I plan to marry her and
remain here when my tour is over. I know we made plans for
our lives together, but I now know it wasn't meant to be. I
hope you find all the happiness you deserve. Charles."

                                        (CONTINUED)

BACK TO SCENE

Vivian's eyes glisten. She closes her eyes as she refolds
the letter and inserts it back into the envelope. She lays
her head against the back of the chair and stares at the
sunset in silent contemplation.

57   INT. VIVIAN'S BAKE SHOP - MORNING - NEXT DAY - MONDAY, JULY   57
      6, 1953

The shop is quiet. Vivian sits with Bryce at one of the
tables. A manila folder and papers lay scattered on the
table alongside two coffee cups. Vivian examines one of the
documents as Bryce eats his doughnut.

                    BRYCE
          They were impressed with your
          businesses plan, but that's the best
          deal you could get. You'll have to
          put up the bakery, your house, and
          your car as collateral.

                    VIVIAN
          That's everything I own! And, six
          and a half percent interest seems
          awful high.

                    BRYCE
          You're lucky you got that. Not many
          banks want to give a business loan
          to a woman. Oh, and, you'll have to
          relocate to St. Louis.

She places the document on the table. Bryce holds out a
pen. Vivian looks around at her bake shop as she contemplates
her options.

58   INT. MOTEL COFFEE SHOP   58

Scotty enters. Lorraine already has his coffee and muffin
waiting for him. Scotty is in a cheerful mood. Doris works
in the background.

                    SCOTTY
          Mornin' boss! Mornin' Doris.

Lorraine smirks at him. Scotty LAUGHS. Doris waves.

                    LORRAINE
          Carl tells me its pretty quiet around
          the garage.

Scotty nods and sits down at the counter.

                                              (CONTINUED)

                    SCOTTY
          Mostly just gas and some flats.
          Nothing Carl can't handle.

                    LORRAINE
          Good. Because Doris can cover for
          me and you can give me one of those
          driving lessons.

Scotty's expression turns to a combination of fear and
reluctance.

                    SCOTTY
          Are you sure you want to start today?
          What if...

Lorraine just shakes her head signaling to Scotty he need
not finish his sentence. He SIGHS a deep sigh. Lorraine
pats him on the forearm.

                    LORRAINE
          Come on. It's not like you're going
          to war.

Scotty rolls his eyes.

Lorraine stands in the doorway and with a sweep of her hand
invites Scotty to join her. Scotty gets up slowly and ambles
over to her. They exit.

59   EXT. MAIN STREET (ROUTE 66) MAPLE GROVE - MOMENTS LATER   59

Vivian drives up a side road adjacent to Main Street. She
approaches a stop light at the Main Street intersection just
in time to see the Hanke's car cross the intersection with
Scotty and Lorraine. Scotty is driving.

Vivian turns and follows hoping to catch up with them at
their destination.

VIVIAN

Vivian's expression turns to curiosity when they pass all
the usual destinations. Her curiosity is further piqued
when they drive to the edge of town and turn down a remote
tree-lined dirt road.

BACK TO SCENE

Vivian follows at a discreet distance. Ed and Lorraine
continue about a 1/4 of a mile and then turn onto another
dirt road that crosses a large open field. They stop.

Vivian stops near a grove of trees and watches.

                              (CONTINUED)

VIVIAN'S POV

Ed and Lorraine sit in the car for a moment. Vivian cannot
see what is happening. For a moment her expression turns
from curiosity to suspicion.

BACK TO SCENE

They both get out of the car and switch places. Lorraine
gets in the driver's side and closes the door. Scotty stands
alongside giving Lorraine some kind of direction and points
down the dirt road.

VIVIAN

A broad grin crosses Vivian's face as she realizes what is
happening.

BACK TO SCENE

The car starts to buck and creep forward. Scotty holds out
his hands in exasperation indicating for Lorraine to stop.
The car bucks and stalls. He goes to window and explains
something else, then walks around the car and gets in the
passenger side. The car bucks again and creeps slowly down
the road.

VIVIAN

Vivian presses her hands to her face and CHUCKLES at Scotty's
predicament. She turns her car around and drives away.

60   EXT. VIVIAN'S BAKE SHOP - MOMENTS LATER   60

Vivian arrives at the shop and parks out front.

61   INT. VIVIAN'S BAKE SHOP   61

Vivian enters. Clarice is behind the counter.

                         CLARICE
                  Errands all done?

                         VIVIAN
                    (distracted)
                  Hi Clarice, I'm back.

The response seems a little odd, but Clarice ignores it and
continues about her work. Vivian walks around the shop in
contemplation and then sits at a table.

                         VIVIAN (CONT'D)
                  Clarice, do you think you could run
                  the shop if I wasn't around?

                                        (CONTINUED)

                    CLARICE
          Every day?

                    VIVIAN
          Yes, in my place.

                    CLARICE
          Sure. I guess I could. Why? Where
          are you going?

                    VIVIAN
               (coyly)
          Oh, nowhere. But it never hurts to
          have a plan just in case.

Clarice smirks. Vivian sits, deep in thought.

62   INT. VIVIAN'S BAKE SHOP - LATER   62

Clarice works around the counter. Vivian is in the back
baking.

                    VIVIAN (O.S.)
          Clarice, do we have enough jelly
          doughnuts?

Clarice checks the display case.

                    CLARICE
          A dozen or so.

A moment passes. Vivian enters with a tray of brownies and
slides them into a display case.

She sees Scotty and Lorraine park outside. Lorraine leads
Scotty inside. Scotty appears a little drained.

                    VIVIAN
          Good morning!

Scotty drops down on a chair. Lorraine grins as if she has
a secret to tell Vivian.

                    LORRAINE
               (half-whispering)
          Had my first driving lesson!

Vivian observes Scotty's condition.

                    VIVIAN
               (trying to restrain
                her amusement)
          How did it go?

                                             (CONTINUED)

                    LORRAINE
          I think it went pretty well, right
          Scotty?

                    SCOTTY
          Oh yeah. Vivian, could I please get
          some black coffee?

Vivian brings Scotty a cup of coffee and pats him on the
back.

                    VIVIAN
          Maybe you should take the rest of
          the day off.

Scotty nods.

63   INT. VIVIAN'S BAKE SHOP - DUSK   63

     Clarice has gone home for the night and Vivian closes up.
     She flips the "OPEN" sign on the door to "CLOSED".

64   EXT. VIVIAN'S BAKE SHOP   64

     Vivian steps outside and locks the door. She looks around
     and reflects for a moment.

     MONTAGE

     -- Main Street (Route 66) as neon signs begin to glow in the
     twilight.

     -- The marquee of the town movie theater lights up announcing
     its current attraction, "Invaders From Mars".

     BACK TO SCENE

     She gets into her car and drives off.

65   EXT. MAPLE GROVE GAS STATION - MORNING - NEXT DAY - TUESDAY,   65
     JULY 7, 1953

     A bright, sparkling morning in Maple Grove with clear blue
     skies overhead. Scotty arrives at the garage.

     Scotty hears the THRUM of an aircraft and looks up to see
     the old WWII era J-5A Piper Cub Army observation plane. He
     watches with a combination of curiosity and envy until the
     plane is out of sight.

66   INT. MAPLE GROVE GAS STATION - GARAGE - MOMENTS LATER   66

     Scotty enters. Carl is cleaning up the work area.

                                        (CONTINUED)

                    SCOTTY
          Good morning, Carl. What's up?

                    CARL
          Mornin' Mr. Scotty. Kinda quiet.
          Just doin' some cleanin'.

                    SCOTTY
          Carl, do you know anything about
          that old army plane flying around?

                    CARL
          That must be old man Morris. The
          word is he was a pilot in the first
          war. Has a bunch of them machines
          on his farm.

Scotty arches his eyebrows in silent contemplation.

                    SCOTTY
          Hmm.

Ed hobbles in.

                    CARL
          Mr. Hanke! Welcome back!

Scotty places a stool near the workbench for him.

                    SCOTTY
          Looking good, Ed. Have a seat.

                    ED
          Doc said I can do light work and
          drive again.

Ed looks around as he slowly makes his way to the stool.

                    ED (CONT'D)
          How'd you two make out without me?

                    CARL
          We did just fine, boss.

Ed sits and fusses around the workbench.

                    ED
          Cleaned up the place, did ya'?

Ed finds the box behind the toolbox and opens it.

                    ED (CONT'D)
          Hey Scotty, is this that coil you
          needed?

                              (CONTINUED)

                    SCOTTY
          Is that where I left it? Been looking
          for that darn thing.

Ed slides it across the workbench.

                    ED
          Now you'll be able to get the heck
          outta here! Get back to your real
          life.

Scotty's expression reveals he is not anxious to leave.

                    SCOTTY
          Yeah, well, I don't want to miss USO
          Night. I figure I'll stick around
          another day or so.

                    ED
          Glad to hear it! Lorraine said you
          might join us. You'll like the guys
          and the food's always good.

Scotty hesitates.

                    SCOTTY
          Yeah, well, I guess I should get
          this in the car.

Scotty takes the box and exits.

                    ED
          Need any help?

                    SCOTTY (O.S.)
          No, thanks. I can handle it.

67   EXT. CABIN #7 - LATER   67

Scotty sits on the front porch of his cabin contemplating
the future. Eddie rides up on his bicycle.

                    EDDIE
          Hey Mr. Scott, I got some baseball
          cards and clothes pins.

Scotty's concentration is broken. Eddie hops off his bike
and steadies it with the kickstand.

Scotty steps off the porch and Eddie hands him the cards and
clothes pins. Scotty kneels besides the back wheel.

                                             (CONTINUED)

                        SCOTTY
              You bend the card a little at one
              end and put it on the fender support,
              like this.

SCOTTY, EDDIE AND BICYCLE

Scotty places a card on the fender support so that it sticks
into the spokes.

                     SCOTTY (CONT'D)
              Then you clip a clothes pin on the
              support to hold it.

Scotty clips the card to the support. He lifts the back of
the bike and spins the wheel. The card against the spokes
makes a CLACKETY sound as the wheel spins. Scotty lowers
the bike back on the ground.

                     SCOTTY (CONT'D)
              Now you put one on the other side
              and some on the front wheel.

Eddie gets to work as Scotty sits on the ground and watches.

BACK TO SCENE

The sun is starting to set and the sky is turning a bright
orange as Eddie finishes his work. Scotty gets to his feet
and Eddie jumps on his bike.

Eddie rides around in front of the cabin as Scotty watches.
The bike makes a CLACKING sound as the wheels spin.

                        EDDIE
              Hey, it works!

Scotty smiles as he watches Eddie ride.

68   INT. MOTEL COFFEE SHOP - MORNING - NEXT DAY - WEDNESDAY,   68
       JULY 8, 1953

Lorraine is in her usual spot behind the counter. Doris is
waiting on some customers.

Scotty shows up with an armful of clothes.

                       LORRAINE
                   (cheerfully)
              Good morning!

Scotty appears anxious.

                                               (CONTINUED)

                         SCOTTY
               Morning. Lorraine, I don't have my
               uniform, do you think these will be
               OK?

Scotty shows her his khaki pants, khaki shirt, and his brown
leather flight jacket.

                         LORRAINE
               Those will be fine, sweetie.

                         SCOTTY
               I'll get them cleaned. Do you think
               I need a haircut? I'll get one
               anyway.

                         LORRAINE
               Take Ed and Eddie with you, will
               ya'?

Scotty nods and heads to the door.

                         LORRAINE (CONT'D)
                    (facetiously)
               Hey, who you trying to impress?
               They're just a bunch of old soldiers.

She CHUCKLES and Scotty exits in a rush.

A few moments later a BELL rings signaling someone has entered
the Motel office. Lorraine wipes off her hands and exits to
the office through a connecting hallway.

69   INT. MAPLE GROVE MOTEL OFFICE   69

A delivery MAN2 and delivery MAN3 are waiting for her.
Delivery Man2 has an invoice in hand.

                         LORRAINE
               Good morning, how can I help you?

                         MAN2
               I got an order here for 11 TV's.

                         LORRAINE
               Eleven? It should be only 10.

Man2 checks the invoice.

                         MAN2
               Nope. Ten table tops and a console.

Lorraine purses her lips and shakes her head as she realizes
what Scotty did. She takes the invoice.

                              (CONTINUED)

                    LORRAINE
          Well, OK. Is this the bill?

                    MAN2
          No. I guess they'll send that.

                    LORRAINE
             (skeptically)
          Un huh.

                    MAN2
          We're supposed to install 'em for
          ya'.

                    LORRAINE
          Oh, yes, thank you. One in each
          cabin and the console in the house
          behind the office, please.

                    MAN2
          Yes, ma'am.

                    LORRAINE
          Oh, and when you're done stop in the
          coffee shop next door for something
          to eat if you'd like.

                    MAN2
          Yes, ma'am. Thank you ma'am.

     The two men exit. Lorraine returns to the coffee shop.

70   EXT. MOTEL COFFEE SHOP - MOMENTS LATER   70

     Vivian arrives and sees the delivery truck out front. She
     takes a box of baked goods out of her car. On her way into
     the coffee shop she notices a label on one of the boxes
     sitting next to the truck.

     INSERT LABEL

     which reads, SCOTT ENTERPRISES, NEW YORK and LOS ANGELES.

     BACK TO SCENE

     Her forehead creases with curiosity and she heads inside the
     coffee shop.

71   INT. MOTEL COFFEE SHOP   71

     Vivian enters and places the box on the counter.

                    LORRAINE
          Good morning, sweetheart.

                                        (CONTINUED)

                    VIVIAN
          Good morning Lorraine. What's going
          on out there?

                    LORRAINE
          I was able to get some television
          sets for the motel.

                    VIVIAN
          I thought the budget was little short
          this month.

                    LORRAINE
          I got a good deal.

                    VIVIAN
          Oh, really? That's great.

It's obvious from her tone that Vivian's curiosity has been
aroused. Lorraine just smiles and ignores her. Lorraine
opens the box.

                    LORRAINE
          Everything smells wonderful as usual.

Vivian just glances at Lorraine suspiciously, her forehead
creased, and then helps her to unpack.

72   EXT. VFW POST #2234 - EVENING   72

The parking lot outside the old building is filled with cars.
MEN and WOMEN, many in old military uniforms enter the
building.

Ed and Scotty arrive in the Hanke's car. Ed is dressed in
his army uniform, and Scotty wears his khaki outfit and
leather flight jacket.

73   INT. VFW POST #2234   73

The inside is crowded with veterans and their guests. The
hall is decorated mid-1940's and a band plays swing music
from the war years. Long tables set end-to-end along one
wall hold the buffet for a spaghetti dinner and desserts. A
bar is on the opposite side of the hall.

In the center are round tables and chairs, some already
occupied by guests. In the center of each table is a red,
white, and blue flower arrangement with an American flag.

A dance floor sits between the band on one end of the hall
and the tables. Some of the guests dance to the music while
others sit and eat.

                              (CONTINUED)

Lorraine, Vivian, and the other hostesses dressed in 1940's
War Era USO costume, mingle with the guests and assist with
dinner.

Ed and Scotty enter. Ed is greeted by some of his army
buddies. Lorraine notices them enter and motions to Vivian.

Vivian joins Lorraine as she goes over to greet Scotty and
Ed. Vivian greets Scotty with a smile.

                    VIVIAN
               (playfully)
          Good evening sailor. Welcome to the
          USO. My name is Vivian.

She takes Scotty by the arm. Scotty beams and plays along.
Lorraine ushers Ed.

                    SCOTTY
          Good evening Vivian. You can call
          me Scotty.

                    VIVIAN
          I'm glad you could join us, Scotty.
          We have a table for you right over
          here.

Lorraine and Vivian seat Ed and Scotty at an empty table.

                    SCOTTY
          Vivian, you look sensational.

She smiles.

                    LORRAINE
          Gentlemen, can we get you some dinner?

Scotty is a little uncomfortable with the attention, but
continues to play along.

                    SCOTTY
          Yes, please. Thank you.

Lorraine and Vivian head over to the buffet table.

Three MEN walk up to Scotty and Ed. One wears an Army
uniform, another Marine dress blues, and the third is a MASTER
CHIEF in a Navy uniform. His eyes narrow and he studies
Scotty carefully. Scotty and Ed stand.

Ed introduces the soldier and then the Marine.

                    ED
          Scotty, this is Bill Stepowkski.
               (MORE)

                                        (CONTINUED)

                    ED (CONT'D)
          Served with me in Europe. And Ty
          Drummond. He was with you boys in
          the Pacific. Gentlemen, this is
          Rick Scott. Call him Scotty.

They shake hands with Scotty.

                    ED (CONT'D)
          Now, Mac here...

Before Ed can introduce the Master Chief, he and Scotty
recognize each other. The Master Chief snaps to attention
and salutes.

                    MASTER CHIEF
          --Sir, Master Chief McGivern.

Scotty steps back and returns the salute. The two men
embrace.

                    SCOTTY
          Glad to see you made it home, Mac.

                    MASTER CHIEF
          Wouldn't have if it wasn't for you,
          sir.

                    SCOTTY
          Well, we all did what we had to do.

Ed's curiosity is piqued by the exchange between Scotty and
Mac.

                    ED
          Mac, what's the story here?

                    MASTER CHIEF
          Scotty, Lieutenant Scott, risked his
          life to save his shipmates from a
          Kamikaze attack.

Ed listens intently as the Master Chief tells the story with
animated hand gestures.

LORRAINE AND VIVIAN

notice the action from the buffet line.

                    VIVIAN
          What do you suppose is going on over
          there?

                                        (CONTINUED)

                    LORRAINE
          War stories. Ed has a thousand of
          them.

BACK TO SCENE

The Master Chief finishes his story.

                    MASTER CHIEF
               (to Scotty)
          An honor to have you join us tonight,
          sir.

                    SCOTTY
          The pleasure is all mine, Mac. And,
          we're going to have a problem if you
          don't call me Scotty.

                    MASTER CHIEF
          Sir.

The Master Chief smiles and nods, and then the three men
head to the bar. Scotty sits and takes a deep breath.

                    ED
          Son, you've been holdin' out on me.

Scotty sees Lorraine and Vivian approaching.

                    SCOTTY
          We'll talk later Ed.

Lorraine and Vivian return with dinners for Ed, Scotty, and
themselves. Vivian sits next to Scotty. Just then Bryce
arrives, in uniform, and with his dinner in hand.

                    BRYCE
          There you are. Mind if I join you?

                    SCOTTY
          Please.

Bryce sits on the other side of Vivian. Before Ed can say
anything, Bryce begins.

                    BRYCE
               (to Scotty)
          I see you met Master Chief Mac.
          Nice guy. Post commander. Served
          in the Pacific. If it was anything
          like France in '45, it was rough. I
          remember one time we got stuck in
          the snow for two days. Pretty cold.

                                        (CONTINUED)

Ed rolls his eyes. Scotty and the others just nod and eat
quietly as Bryce tells his stories.

MONTAGE

with the MUSIC of the band in the background.

-- People eating

-- People dancing

-- People talking

BACK TO SCENE

Scotty finishes his dinner. Vivian tries to take his plate,
but Scotty stops her. He takes her plate and gets up.

> SCOTTY
> Dessert?

> VIVIAN
> Surprise me.

Scotty takes the plates to the dish bin. He stops at the
dessert table and puts together a plate of brownies and
cupcakes. He returns and places the plate on the table.

> SCOTTY
> A little something for everyone.

> VIVIAN
> Thank you.

Bryce grabs a cupcake.

> BRYCE
> That was very thoughtful.

The band stops playing and the Master Chief takes the
microphone.

> MASTER CHIEF
> Good evening everyone. May I have
> your attention?

The crowd quiets down.

> MASTER CHIEF
> Good evening, everyone. I want to
> welcome you all to VFW Post 2234 and
> our annual USO night.

The crowd APPLAUDS.

(CONTINUED)

                    MASTER CHIEF (CONT'D)
          For those of you who helped make
          this beautiful evening possible, all
          the veterans and I, thank you.

The crowd APPLAUDS again. The Master Chief pauses to gather
his thoughts.

                    MASTER CHIEF (CONT'D)
          I would also like to personally
          welcome a special guest this evening.
          If it were not for this man, I would
          not be here with you tonight.
          Lieutenant Richard Scott.

Scotty is surprised and embarrassed by the attention, and
reluctantly waves from his seat.

                    MASTER CHIEF (CONT'D)
          Off the coast of Japan in 1945,
          Lieutenant Scott rammed his fighter
          into a Japanese kamikaze before it
          could strike our ship. Without this
          selfless act, many men would have
          never seen their families again.
          Fortunately, Lieutenant Scott
          miraculously survived after 3 months
          in a hospital. He was awarded the
          Medal of Honor for his bravery.
          Sir!

The Master Chief comes to attention and salutes. Ed and
Bryce rise and salute. An old veteran seated at the next
table struggles as he rises from his wheelchair and snaps
his best salute. Lorraine and Vivian watch in awe as all
the veterans in the hall stand, turn toward Scotty and salute.

Scotty rises, choked with emotion, glances around the hall
and returns their salute. The crowd APPLAUDS.

                    MASTER CHIEF (CONT'D)
          Thank you all for coming, and I hope
          you have have a pleasant evening.

And the band begins to play again.

Scotty sits and his eyes meet Vivian's. The display of
respect and gratitude has brought tears to her eyes. She
squeezes Scotty's hand.

Bryce extends his hand to Scotty.

                    BRYCE
          It is a privilege to know you, sir.

                                        (CONTINUED)

Scotty shakes his hand.

>   SCOTTY
>   Scotty.

Bryce nods. There is an awkward silence at the table.

>   VIVIAN
>   (to Scotty)
>   Lieutenant. May I have this dance?

She takes Scotty by the hand. He glances at Lorraine, and
she smiles with her hands crossed and pressed against her
chest in a show of emotion. Vivian leads Scotty to the dance
floor.

As they make their way through the crowd veterans reach out
to shake his hand.

DANCE FLOOR

The band is playing a slow song (i.e., Moonlight Serenade).
He takes Vivian in his arms. She says nothing and looks
into his eyes. They dance slowly, swaying to the music.

>   SCOTTY
>   I didn't think it was important.

>   VIVIAN
>   Some men would try to impress a girl
>   with a story like that.

Scotty shrugs.

>   SCOTTY
>   Vivian, there's something else I
>   need to tell you.

>   VIVIAN
>   Oh? What's that?

>   SCOTTY
>   It's about my job.

She cocks her head.

>   VIVIAN
>   Oh, you mean Scott Enterprises, yes,
>   I know.

Vivian CHUCKLES in response to the surprise on Scotty's face.

>   (CONTINUED)

                    VIVIAN (CONT'D)
          I noticed the label on the boxes at
          the motel and did a little research.
          Why didn't you want me to know?

                    SCOTTY
          I wanted you to know the real me
          first. I'm just a simple guy from a
          small town.

                    VIVIAN
          Who still likes baseball and cars.

They LAUGH.

                    VIVIAN (CONT'D)
          I like who you are either way. And
          I'm glad you came home safely.

A moment passes as they dance.

                    SCOTTY
          Vivian, can I ask you something?

                    VIVIAN
          What did Bryce mean about my past?

Scotty nods. Tears fill her eyes. She pauses.

                    VIVIAN (CONT'D)
          I was engaged to a soldier, who was
          assigned to the occupation forces in
          Japan. After about six months, he
          wrote and told me he found someone
          else in Japan. I guess I wasn't
          what...

Scotty interrupts her. He doesn't want her to relive the
past. He gazes into her eyes.

                    SCOTTY
          --There were days in the hospital,
          when I thought the pain would never
          go away. But I'd gladly do it all
          over again, if I knew it would lead
          me to be here, with you, tonight.

Vivian is deeply moved by Scotty's passionate declaration of
affection. Her eyes fill. She kisses him on the cheek and
lays her head on his shoulder.

SERIES OF SHOTS

Scotty and Vivian dance the night away until the band stops
playing and they notice people are leaving.

                                             (CONTINUED)

BACK TO SCENE

Scotty and Vivian return to the table where Ed is preparing
to leave.

                    LORRAINE
          (to Ed)
     I'll be just a little while. I have
     to help clean up here.

                    ED
          (to Scotty)
     Let's go sailor, unless you wanna
     hoof it.

                    SCOTTY
     Lorraine, you go with Ed. I'll help
     Vivian clean up.

                    VIVIAN
     Go ahead Lorraine. I'll give him a
     ride.

Lorraine smiles and winks at Vivian. Vivian just smirks at
her. Lorraine follows Ed out the door.

On his way out, Old Man MORRIS stops to shake Scotty's hand.

                    MORRIS
     The name is Morris, Jed Morris. I
     flew in the first war. You're a
     good man, son. Stop by my farm
     sometime and I'll show you some fine
     airplanes.

                    SCOTTY
     Will do. Thank you sir. Nice to
     meet you sir.

Morris shuffles out the door. Scotty helps Vivian and the
other ladies clean up.

74   EXT. CABIN #7 - LATER   74

Vivian's car pulls up in front of the cabin.

75   INT. VIVIAN'S CAR   75

Scotty and Vivian sit in awkward silence for a moment. She
turns and gazes into his eyes.

                    VIVIAN
     Thank you for a wonderful evening.
     And thank you, for watching over my
     sister and her family.

                              (CONTINUED)

Scotty is caught up in her gaze and doesn't respond. Vivian
leans over and kisses him, a sweet, gentle kiss on the lips.
Scotty is bewitched. All he can manage is a whisper.

                    SCOTTY
          Good night.

                    VIVIAN
          Good night.

Scotty takes her hand and kisses it.

76   EXT. CABIN #7   76

Scotty gets out of the car and watches Vivian drive away.

77   INT. MOTEL COFFEE SHOP - MORNING - NEXT DAY - THURSDAY, JULY   77
     9, 1953

Scotty is a little later than usual getting to the coffee
shop and Eddie is already waiting for him. Eddie eats his
breakfast at the counter and Lorraine stands watching him.

Scotty enters. Eddie jumps to attention and salutes. Scotty
returns the salute.

                    SCOTTY
          As you were.

                    EDDIE
          What?

                    SCOTTY
          Finish your breakfast.

Scotty sits next to Eddie.

                    EDDIE
               (excited)
          Mr. Scott, dad says you're a pilot!
          Are you a pilot? Are you?

Lorraine smiles.

                    SCOTTY
          Yes sir. I'm a pilot.

                    EDDIE
          No foolin'? That's the coolest!

                    LORRAINE
          Eddie. Slow down. Let Mr. Scott
          eat his breakfast.

                                        (CONTINUED)

Eddie scowls, but sits quietly. Lorraine brings Scotty his
cup of coffee. She places a tray of doughnuts and muffins
near him. He grabs a muffin.

                    LORRAINE (CONT'D)
          Must have been quite a night, Vivian
          took the day off.

                    SCOTTY
          Tommy Boyd's an idiot.

Lorraine squints at him. She doesn't understand.

                    SCOTTY (CONT'D)
          You can go home again, and it can be
          better that you ever imagined.

Lorraine smiles and pats him on the arm. Eddie can't restrain
himself any longer.

                    EDDIE
          Can you take me flying? Can you
          teach me how to fly? Dad says you
          flew fighter planes!

                    SCOTTY
          Well, Mr. Morris invited me over to
          see his airplanes. Maybe, if you
          finish your breakfast, and it's OK
          with your mother, you can come with
          me.

                    EDDIE
          No foolin'? Can I go Ma, can I go?

Lorraine points to Eddie's breakfast.

                    LORRAINE
          Finish!
               (looking at Scotty)
          If you're careful.

                    SCOTTY
          Yes, ma'am. Understood!

                    EDDIE
          Oh cool. I'm gonna fly.

Lorraine points to his breakfast. Eddie eats.

                    LORRAINE
          You're two of my favorite guys so...

                    SCOTTY
          --I promise to be careful.

                              (CONTINUED)

Scotty has barely finished his breakfast when Eddie jumps
off his stool

                         EDDIE
               Finished!

He stares at Scotty. Scotty wipes his hands with a napkin,
takes a last sip of coffee, and gets up.

                         SCOTTY
               Let's go!

Eddie runs out the door ahead of him. Scotty smiles at
Lorraine.

                         SCOTTY (CONT'D)
               Baseball, cars, and, airplanes!

Lorraine arches her eyebrows and shakes her finger at Scotty.

                         SCOTTY (CONT'D)
               I promise!

He follows Eddie out the door.

78   INT. VIVIAN'S HOUSE   78

Vivian stands in the kitchen, the old envelope in hand. She
starts to remove the letter and then stops.

79   EXT. VIVIAN'S HOUSE - BACK PORCH   79

Vivian walks out the back door carrying the envelope, descends
the stairs and walks up to a rusty 50 gallon drum. She takes
one last look at the envelope and lights it with a match.
She tosses it into the drum and returns inside her house.

80   EXT. MORRIS FARM   80

Scotty drives his car down a dusty dirt road that leads to
the Morris farm. The farm is a spacious landscape of
seemingly endless open fields dotted with groves of trees.
The farm includes a farmhouse surrounded by two barns and an
old, aircraft hangar. Scotty parks alongside the farmhouse.

Scotty and Eddie get out of the car and look around, but see
no one.

81   EXT. MORRIS FARM - HANGAR   81

Morris appears in front of the hangar and calls to them.

                         MORRIS
               Over here!

                                        (CONTINUED)

Scotty waves, and he and Eddie walk over to the hangar.
Inside the hangar are two airplanes - an AT6 Texan training
aircraft painted in the Navy yellow and blue, and the J-5A
Piper Cub Army Observation plane with the Army colors and
Victory stripes.

Eddie is itching to get a closer look but remains by Scotty's
side. Scotty shakes hands with Morris.

                    SCOTTY
          Good morning, sir.

                    MORRIS
          Mornin' son. Who's your co-pilot?

                    SCOTTY
          Mr. Morris, this is my friend, Eddie.
          Eddie, this is Mr. Morris.

Eddie shakes hands with Morris.

                    EDDIE
          Nice to meet you sir.

                    MORRIS
          Good manners. I like that.

This is way too much talking for Eddie and he can't take his
eyes off the planes.

                    MORRIS (CONT'D)
          Fine evening last night. The young
          lady you were with sure was a looker.

                    SCOTTY
          Prettiest girl at the party. Made
          all the desserts.

                    MORRIS
          She's a keeper!
              (turning to the planes)
          Well, these are my girls. Tip-top
          shape.

Eddie runs into the hangar. Scotty and Morris follow.

Scotty examines the Texan. He looks up at the cockpit.

                    SCOTTY
          May I?

                    MORRIS
          Climb aboard.

Scotty hops up onto the wing and slips into the cockpit.

                              (CONTINUED)

                    SCOTTY
          Looks like new in here.

                    MORRIS
          Tip-top shape.

Eddie is dying to get into the plane, his eyes darting between
Morris and the plane. Morris notices.

                    MORRIS (CONT'D)
               (to Eddie)
          Climb aboard, son!

Morris boosts Eddie onto the wing and Eddie climbs into the
back seat. Eddie is wide-eyed.

                    EDDIE
          Can you fly this, Mr. Scott?

                    SCOTTY
          Learned to fly in one of these.

Scotty looks over the cockpit for a moment and then climbs
out.

                    SCOTTY (CONT'D)
               (to Eddie)
          Let's go check out the Cub.

Eddie frowns a bit, but climbs out. Scotty jumps down off
the wing and then assists Eddie. They walk over to the Piper
Cub along with Morris.

                    MORRIS
          This is my sweetheart. Easy to fly
          and a smooth ride.

Scotty walks around the plane examining it as if performing
a pre-flight inspection. Scotty's diligence is not lost on
Morris.

                    SCOTTY
          She's a beauty.

                    MORRIS
          All fueled up and ready to go.

Scotty looks at Morris, silently questioning if Morris is
serious.

                    MORRIS (CONT'D)
          Go ahead. And take your co-pilot.

Eddie is not exactly sure what is going on, but slowly figures
it out.

                              (CONTINUED)

                    EDDIE
          No foolin'! Can we Mr. Scott, can
          we?

Scotty looks at the plane, then Morris, and then Eddie who
has his hands clasped in a praying position.

                    SCOTTY
          Let's fly!

82   INT. VIVIAN'S HOUSE   82

Vivian is cleaning up in the kitchen. Her baseball mitt is
on the counter.

83   EXT. SKIES OVER MAPLE GROVE   83

Scotty and Eddie are airborne and cruise through the clear
blue sky.

84   INT. J-5A PIPER CUB   84

Eddie sits in the back seat and Scotty pilots the aircraft
from the front seat. Eddie and Scotty are wearing headsets
so they can communicate over the THRUM of the plane's engine.

                    SCOTTY
          There's the motel.

Scotty banks over the motel.

                    EDDIE
          Cool.

They cruise for a few moments.

                    EDDIE (CONT'D)
          Hey, that looks like Aunt Vivian's
          house.

Eddie points over Scotty's shoulder. Scotty banks and looks.

                    SCOTTY
          Sure looks like her car.

                    EDDIE
          That's it! That's it!

                    SCOTTY
          Whattaya say we stop in for a visit?

                    EDDIE
          Cool!

                                        (CONTINUED)

Scotty banks the plane. He reduces the power and prepares
to land in the field behind Vivian's house.

85   INT. VIVIAN'S HOUSE   85

Vivian hears the THRUM of an airplane getting closer and
closer. She looks out a back window and sees the plane
getting lower and lower.

86   EXT. VIVIAN'S HOUSE - BACK PORCH   86

Vivian rushes out onto the back porch. She slowly descends
the steps into her back yard, and watches the plane touch
down and come to a stop. She stands there with a confused
squint and her hands on her hips.

The door swings open and Eddie hops out. Scotty follows.
Her expression changes from confusion to a broad grin. Eddie
runs over to her.

                    VIVIAN
          What are you two up to?!

                    EDDIE
          I've been flying. Mr. Scott took me
          flying!

She hugs him.

                    VIVIAN
          I see that.

Scotty walks over and just looks at her with a thin smile,
unsure what to do next. Vivian kisses him on the cheek.

                    VIVIAN (CONT'D)
          Good morning.

Scotty smiles.

                    SCOTTY
          Good morning.

                    VIVIAN
          Did Lorraine approve this?

Scotty nods with an expression of disbelief.

                    SCOTTY
          She did.

He looks around at Vivian's house and yard.

                    SCOTTY (CONT'D)
          Nice home you have here.

                              (CONTINUED)

                    VIVIAN
               (proudly)
          I built it! I bought the kit as a
          surprise for my fiancee, when he...
          Well, I had some help from Ed and
          the others, but I built it.

Scotty nods.

                    SCOTTY

          Good job!

                    EDDIE
          Hey Mr. Scott, lets fly some more.
          Aunt Vivian, it is so cool. You can
          see the whole world from up there.

                    VIVIAN
          I'll bet you can, and its a beautiful
          day for flying.

                    SCOTTY
          It's a 3 seater.

                    VIVIAN
          What?

                    SCOTTY
          It's a 3 seater.

Vivian gets his message, but is hesitant.

                    VIVIAN
          Oh, I don't know.

                    EDDIE
          C'mon Aunt Vivian, it's a blast!

Scotty looks her square in the eye.

                    SCOTTY
          Don't you trust me?

Vivian takes a deep breath and exhales.

                    VIVIAN
          OK, let's go.

Eddie runs over to the plane. Scotty and Vivian follow.

Eddie jumps into the back seat. Vivian slides in next to
him, and Scotty helps her put on a headset and seat belt.
He climbs into the front seat and FIRES up the engine.

                                        (CONTINUED)

He swings the plane around. The plane RUMBLES across the field and lifts into the air.

87   INT. J-5A PIPER CUB   87

Vivian leans forward in her seat with one hand locked on the back of Scotty's seat, and the other in a death grip on his shoulder as the plane climbs and gently banks.

                         VIVIAN
            Easy now. No fancy pilot stuff.

Scotty CHUCKLES.

                         EDDIE
            Mr. Scott, can you make this roll
            over like in the movies?

                         VIVIAN
            Edward!

The plane levels out and cruises through the clear blue sky. Vivian begins to relax as she looks out the window at the landscape below.

                         VIVIAN (CONT'D)
            This is beautiful.

                         SCOTTY
            This is what I like to do when the
            world gets too crazy. Everything
            seems clearer up here.

Scotty banks the plane.

                         SCOTTY (CONT'D)
            There's your bake shop.

                         VIVIAN
            Yes, there it is.

MONTAGE

-- they fly through a cloudless blue sky.

88   EXT. VIVIAN'S HOUSE - BACK YARD - LATER   88

The plane is parked in the field behind the house. Eddie sits in the front seat pretending to fly on some daring mission.

Scotty sits at a picnic table. Vivian brings out a tray with glasses and a pitcher of lemonade, and sets it on the table. She pours 3 glasses.

                                           (CONTINUED)

                    VIVIAN
          Eddie, there's lemonade here for
          you.

He waves, but continues his mission. She sits next to Scotty
as he sips his lemonade.

                    VIVIAN (CONT'D)
          Thank you for making me try that.
          It was fun.

                    SCOTTY
          I just provided the plane and the
          pilot. I don't think you're the
          kind of girl who does anything she
          doesn't want to do.

She smirks at him.

                    SCOTTY (CONT'D)
          But I'm glad you did. I've never
          been able to share that with anyone
          before. Thank you.

Vivian studies him for a moment.

                    VIVIAN
          I can't help thinking how beautiful
          and peaceful that was today. But,
          it must have been terrifying when
          you crashed into that plane. What
          were you thinking?

Scotty looks at her with a thoughtful gaze.

                    SCOTTY
          Christmas.

She cocks her head with a confused squint. Scotty smiles
and explains.

                    SCOTTY (CONT'D)
          When I was a kid, Christmas was so
          important to my family. It was a
          time of great joy in my life.
                    (he pauses in
                     reflection)
          All I could think of was, that there
          were a lot of men who would never
          again spend Christmas with their
          families, if I didn't do something.
          My life or theirs.

Tears well up in her eyes.

                                             (CONTINUED)

                    SCOTTY (CONT'D)
          Crazy, huh?

She is too choked to speak. She kisses him just as Eddie
arrives at the table.

                    EDDIE
          Oh, yuck. You kissed Aunt Vivian!

                    SCOTTY
               (sarcastically)
          Good timing, buddy.

Vivian LAUGHS. She grabs Eddie and starts kissing him.

                    EDDIE
          Aw, c'mon Aunt Vivian. Yuck!

                    SCOTTY
          My little friend, you have a lot to
          learn.

Eddie doesn't understand. Vivian hands him some lemonade
and turns her attention back to Scotty.

                    VIVIAN
          Mr. Scott, you are an unusual man.

                    SCOTTY
          Is that good?

                    VIVIAN
          It's not bad.

He takes her hand again.

                    SCOTTY
          So, I have a chance?

Vivian is haunted by the past, but cannot deny the the strong
connection with Scotty. She nods weakly with a half smile
and hugs him.

89   INT. MOTEL COFFEE SHOP - LATER   89

Lorraine works behind the counter. Eddie bursts in the door
and Scotty follows.

                    EDDIE
          Mom, mom, we did it. We went flying.
          It was a blast. We flew over the
          motel and landed at Aunt Vivian's
          house and she went flying with us
          and everything.
               (MORE)

                                        (CONTINUED)

                         EDDIE (CONT'D)
               It was so cool, except when Aunt
               Vivian kissed Mr. Scott, that was
               yucky, but it was so cool.

                         SCOTTY
               I liked that part.

Lorraine looks at Scotty with arched brow.

                         LORRAINE
               Had fun did ya?

Scotty grins.

90   INT. CORPORATE OFFICE OF SCOTT ENTERPRISES - NEXT DAY -   90
     FRIDAY, JULY 10, 1953

Tommy Boyd works at his desk. The phone RINGS. He picks it
up and finds HANK BIDWELL on the other end.

                         TOMMY
               Tom Boyd, Scott Enterprises.

                         BIDWELL (V.O.)
               Mr. Boyd, Hank Bidwell from Bidwell
               Property Management in L.A.

                         TOMMY
               Good morning, Mr. Bidwell. I hope
               all is well in Los Angeles.

                         BIDWELL (V.O.)
               Just wondering, where's your boy?

                         TOMMY
               Mr. Scott is on his way. Got hung
               up with a little car trouble.

                         BIDWELL (V.O.)
               Car trouble! He's driving?

                         TOMMY
               It's a long story. What can I do
               for you?

                         BIDWELL (V.O.)
               Well, we need to close that deal. I
               got a bunch of companies interested
               in that building.

                         TOMMY
               The agreement was August first.
               He'll be there.

                                             (CONTINUED)

                    BIDWELL (V.O.)
          I have to tell you, I'm getting some
          offers that are hard to refuse.

                    TOMMY
          A lotta people will be out of a job
          if we don't get that building!

                    BIDWELL (V.O.)
          That's not my problem. Nothing
          personal, just business.

Tommy scowls.

91   INT. VIVIAN'S BAKE SHOP   91

Vivian is in the back and Clarice works out front.

A DELIVERY MAN2 enters with a basket of red and white flowers,
and an envelope in the center of the arrangement.

                    CLARICE
          Vivian!

Vivian enters.

                    CLARICE (CONT'D)
          I know they're not for me.

The Delivery Man2 checks the envelope.

                    DELIVERY MAN2
          I have flowers for a Slugger Donnelly?

Vivian smiles.

                    VIVIAN
          That's me.

The Delivery Man2 is bewildered.

                    DELIVERY MAN2
          You're Slugger?

Vivian nods with raised brows. She takes the flowers and
tips the Delivery Man2. He exits.

Vivian places the flowers on one of the tables. She opens
the envelope and reads the card with Clarice looking over
her shoulder.

                                        (CONTINUED)

INSERT CARD

which reads, "Please accept these 3 tickets for the St. Louis -
Yankees game for you and two of your friends as your prize
for your Home Run Derby Championship. A devoted admirer!"

BACK TO SCENE

Vivian smiles and slips the card back into the envelope.

                    CLARICE
          I guess I'm working tomorrow.

                    VIVIAN
          Do you mind?

                    CLARICE
          Of course not. Funny how things can
          change in a few days.

There is a gentle TAPPING on the window. They look over and
see Scotty spying in the window. Vivian motions for him to
come in.

Clarice heads back to work.

                    CLARICE (CONT'D)
          You were either a very good girl, or
          a very bad girl!

Vivian is shocked, her mouth falls open.

                    VIVIAN
          Clarice! Please!

Clarice smiles coyly at Scotty as they pass each other.

                    VIVIAN (CONT'D)
               (to Scotty)
          You'll never guess. An admirer sent
          me 3 tickets for the St. Louis -
          Yankee game.

Scotty eyebrows rise.

                    SCOTTY
          So, who are you going to take?

                    VIVIAN
          Well, Eddie would never forgive me
          if I didn't take him.

                    SCOTTY
          Of course.

                                        (CONTINUED)

Vivian teases Scotty as she thinks out loud.

                    VIVIAN
          Bryce is probably busy at the bank.

Scotty is not amused. He pouts. Vivian LAUGHS.

                    VIVIAN (CONT'D)
          Would you like to go?

Scotty smirks and kisses her on the cheek.

Clarice brings two cups of coffee for Scotty and Vivian.
They sit.

                    VIVIAN (CONT'D)
              (to Scotty)
          Thank you. And, Eddie will be over
          the moon!

                    SCOTTY
          I can't wait to see his face.

                    VIVIAN
          You're very fond of him aren't you?

                    SCOTTY
          I am. Two weeks ago I was alone.
          Now I feel like I'm part of something
          important, even if it is for just a
          few days.

                    VIVIAN
          He thinks you're pretty special,
          too.
              (a beat)
          You like it here in Maple Grove,
          don't you?

Scotty nods. He takes her hands and gazes into her eyes.

                    SCOTTY
          I love everything about it.

Vivian is a little flustered. Her face turns pink. She
gathers herself.

                    VIVIAN
          So, what happens when you have to
          leave?

                    SCOTTY
          I've got two weeks. I'll deal with
          that when the time comes.

                                        (CONTINUED)

Scotty's response is not very reassuring to Vivian, and the disappointment shows on her face.

                    SCOTTY (CONT'D)
          It'll all work out. I promise.

She's heard the words before, but Scotty's optimism eases her apprehension a bit and she manages a smile.

92   INT. MOTEL COFFEE SHOP - LATER   92

Scotty enters. Lorraine is working behind the counter.
Eddie is trying his best to sweep the floor.

                    SCOTTY
          Hey Eddie. Aunt Vivian got tickets
          for the St. Louis - Yankee game.

Eddie's eyes grow wide.

                    SCOTTY (CONT'D)
          Would you like to go with Aunt Vivian
          and me?

He looks at Lorraine.

                    EDDIE
          Can I mom? Can I?

Lorraine smiles.

                    LORRAINE
          Yes, of course you can go.

Scotty gives him a thumbs up.

                    LORRAINE (CONT'D)
               (to Scotty)
          Oh, you had a telephone call from a
          Tom Boyd. Wants you to call him
          right away. Said it was pretty
          important.

Lorraine hands Scotty a message. Scotty frowns.

93   EXT. BUSCH STADIUM - ST. LOUIS - AFTERNOON - NEXT DAY -   93
     SATURDAY, JULY 11, 1953

The St. Louis Cardinals are playing the New York Yankees.
Scotty, Vivian, and Eddie make their way into the park.
Scotty wears his Yankee cap. Eddie carries his mitt.

94   INT. BUSCH STADIUM   94

MONTAGE

-- Eddie gets to meet some of the St. Louis players.

-- Eddie and Vivian get St. Louis caps, and Eddie gets a St.
Louis pennant.

-- Baseball game.

-- Scotty, Vivian, and Eddie cheering in the stands.

95   INT. SCOTTY'S CAR - EVENING   95

Eddie is asleep in the back seat on the way home. Scotty
drives with Vivian alongside.

                    VIVIAN
          It was sweet of you to arrange all
          that.

                    SCOTTY
          Just seeing Eddie's face was worth
          the trip.

Scotty glances at her and smiles.

                    SCOTTY (CONT'D)
          Sharing it with you made it even
          better.

                    VIVIAN
          I wouldn't have missed it.
               (a beat)
          Can't imagine what you've planned
          next.

Scotty pauses. There's something on his mind.

                    SCOTTY
          Vivian, there's been a change in
          plans. I have to go back to St.
          Louis tomorrow and catch a flight to
          Los Angeles.

He catches Vivian by surprise.

                    VIVIAN
          How long will you be gone?

                    SCOTTY
          Hard to tell, but no longer than I
          have to.

                                        (CONTINUED)

Scotty sees the disappointment and trepidation in her eyes.

                    SCOTTY (CONT'D)
          A lot of people are counting on me.

Vivian stares straight ahead and responds without emotion.

                    VIVIAN
          Of course, I understand.

He squeezes her hand.

                    SCOTTY
          It'll be alright. I'll be back soon.

Vivian nods and manages a weak smile. She stares out the
side window.

96   INT. VIVIAN'S BAKE SHOP - MORNING - ABOUT 2 WEEKS LATER   96

Clarice is working behind the counter when Bryce saunters
in.

                    BRYCE
          Good morning, Clarice. Can I get a
          cup of coffee and a jelly doughnut?

                    CLARICE
          Good morning, Mr. Townsend. Sure.
          Haven't seen you for awhile. Where
          you been?

                    BRYCE
          Busy at the bank.

Clarice hands him the coffee and doughnut. He begins to
leave just as Vivian enters from the back.

                    BRYCE (CONT'D)
          Good morning, Vivian.

                    VIVIAN
          Good morning, Bryce. Nice to see
          you.

The conversation stalls.

                    BRYCE
          Haven't seen Mr. Scott around for a
          couple weeks.

                    VIVIAN
          He had to go to Los Angeles on
          business. He'll be back as soon as
          he can.

                              (CONTINUED)

Bryce decides to sit and stoke Vivian's insecurity.

                    BRYCE
          Is that what he told you?

Vivian grows anxious.

                    VIVIAN
          Yes! He'll be back!

                    BRYCE
          C'mon Vivian. Wise up! You've been
          down this road before.

Vivian glares at him.

                    BRYCE (CONT'D)
          Don't get mad at me. Listen, that
          deal won't be available for much
          longer. If you want to give it a
          try, I'll still be here for you if
          it doesn't work out.

Vivian turns away from him. Tears fill her eyes.

                    VIVIAN
          He'll be back!

She stares out the window.

97   INT. MOTEL COFFEE SHOP - MORNING   97

Another two weeks has passed. Vivian sits at the counter
talking with Lorraine who is standing behind the counter.
Vivian wears a look of disappointment.

                    VIVIAN
          Scotty called last night. Said it
          was going to take longer than he
          thought. He said he would let me
          know.

                    LORRAINE
          It's only been a month. There's a
          lot to running a big company.

Tears fill Vivian's eyes.

                    VIVIAN
          What if he doesn't come back? What
          if he's changed his mind? It's
          happened before! Los Angeles is a
          big city with a lot of pretty girls.

Lorraine rushes around the counter and clasps Vivian's hands.

                              (CONTINUED)

                    LORRAINE
          Not this time! Not Scotty. He loves
          you!

                    VIVIAN
          He loves Maple Grove.

                    LORRAINE
          You are Maple Grove and everything
          he's dreamed of. He won't let you
          down.

Vivian is scarred by the past and shakes her head.

                    VIVIAN
          Bryce says I have to make a decision.
          It's now or never if I want that
          loan. I have to think of my future.

Lorraine pleads with Vivian.

                    LORRAINE
          There must be another way! Call
          Scotty and tell him how you feel!

                    VIVIAN
          And what if he doesn't care? I'd
          feel like a fool.

Lorraine walks over and picks up the receiver for the
telephone. She holds it out to Vivian.

                    LORRAINE
               (sternly)
          Vivian! Call him!

Vivian reluctantly takes the phone.

98   INT. SCOTTY'S NEW OFFICE - LOS ANGELES   98

Scotty is poring over some paperwork on his desk. His new,
young secretary, FRANCINE, enters, but he is too occupied to
notice her.

                    FRANCINE
               Mr. Scott.
                  (a beat)
               Mr. Scott!

Scotty's concentration is broken.

                    SCOTTY
          Oh, Francine, sorry.

                                             (CONTINUED)

                    FRANCINE
          You need to take a break.

                    SCOTTY
          No. I need to get this done today!

He leans back in his chair and rubs the back of his neck.
Francine slips around behind him and massages his shoulders.

                    FRANCINE
          Why don't you stick around? You
          might learn to like L.A. I know a
          nice quiet restaurant. Why don't we
          slip out early and you can take me
          to dinner?

Scotty is oblivious to her overtures.

                    SCOTTY
          No. I leaving here tomorrow, one
          way or another. Mr. Boyd can clean
          up the details.

Francine stops massaging his shoulders and scowls. Scotty
rises with papers in hand and heads to the door.

                    SCOTTY (CONT'D)
          I'm taking these to legal.

He exits. Francine tidies up his office. The phone RINGS
and Francine picks it up.

                    FRANCINE
          Scott Enterprises. Mr. Scott's
          office.

                    VIVIAN (V.O.)
          Oh, hello. This is Vivian Donnelly.
          I would like to speak with Mr. Scott,
          please.

Francine rolls her eyes.

                    FRANCINE
               (coldly)
          Oh, yes. One moment.

Francine holds her hand over the receiver with a devious
smile. A moment passes and she responds to Vivian.

                    FRANCINE (CONT'D)
          I'm sorry. He'll get back to you
          when he can.
               (a beat)
          Goodbye.

                                        (CONTINUED)

She grins wickedly and hangs up.

99   INT. MOTEL COFFEE SHOP   99

Vivian's eyes fill.

                    VIVIAN
          Thank you.

Vivian hands the phone back to Lorraine. Lorraine sees the
tears in Vivian's eyes.

                    LORRAINE
          What's wrong!?

Vivian composes herself.

                    VIVIAN
          She sounded cute.
             (a beat)
          He's too busy to talk to me.

                    LORRAINE
          No! There must be some mistake.
          Call him back!

                    VIVIAN
          No! I have to do this. I have to
          do this before I change my mind.
          I've already made the plans. I'm
          leaving tomorrow.
             (she pauses)
          Please, Lorraine don't call him.
          Please?

Lorraine agrees reluctantly with a nod.

                    VIVIAN (CONT'D)
          I'll call you when I get settled.
          Good bye.

They hug. Vivian kisses Lorraine on the cheek and exits.
Lorraine fidgets around for a few minutes and then picks up
the phone. She DIALS.

                    FRANCINE (V.O.)
          Scott Enterprises. Mr. Scott's
          office.

Lorraine HANGS up. There's a small chance Vivian may be
right.

Eddie enters and sees his mother is unhappy. He hugs her.

                                        (CONTINUED)

                    EDDIE
              What's wrong, mom?

There are tears in her eyes.

                    LORRAINE
              You like Mr. Scott, don't you?

                    EDDIE
              He's my best friend!

Eddie is not sure what is going on, but takes a guess.

                    EDDIE (CONT'D)
              He'll be back, mom. We're going
              flying.

She hugs him.

100   EXT. VIVIAN'S HOUSE - MORNING   100

Vivian packs her suitcase in the car. A "For Sale" sign
hangs in front of the house.

A moving truck sits out front. The DRIVER approaches Vivian
and hands her an invoice.

                    DRIVER
              We'll hold your things in the
              warehouse until you call for them.

                    VIVIAN
                (weakly)
              Thank you.

He nods, then gets into his truck and drives off leaving
Vivian alone. She looks at her house wistfully one more
time, and then gets in the car and drives away.

101   INT. ST. LOUIS CORPORATE OFFICES OF NAFCO - MORNING - NEXT   101
      DAY

Vivian enters the corporate office of the National Foods
Company sharply dressed and carrying a portfolio. She walks
up to the RECEPTIONIST.

                    RECEPTIONIST
              Good morning.

                    VIVIAN
              Good morning. I'm Vivian Donnelly.
              I have an appointment with Mr. Steen.

The Receptionist checks the appointment calendar.

                              (CONTINUED)

                    RECEPTIONIST
          Oh, yes.

The OFFICE MANAGER enters from the office area and sees
Vivian.

                    OFFICE MANAGER
          Well! Hel - lo! If you can make
          coffee, you got the job!

Vivian scowls.

                    RECEPTIONIST
          Miss Donnelly is not here for the
          secretary position. She's meeting
          with Mr. Steen regarding a new baking
          company.

The Office Manager is taken by surprise.

                    OFFICE MANAGER
               (condescendingly)
          Imagine that. Well sweetheart, when
          that doesn't work out, I'll find a
          place for you.

                    VIVIAN
          Lucky me.

The Office Manger scowls and exits.

                    RECEPTIONIST
          Mr. Steen is running late. Have a
          seat and he will be with you as soon
          as he can.

Vivian sits. She checks her watch.

INSERT WATCH

which reads, 8:45

BACK TO SCENE

Vivian reads a magazine as she waits. BUSINESSMEN with
appointments enter and leave, while she waits. She checks
her watch again.

INSERT WATCH

which reads, 10:15

                                        (CONTINUED)

BACK TO SCENE

More time passes. She checks her watch again and pouts. She picks up another magazine, and waits.

102   EXT. SCOTTY'S CAR - AFTERNOON   102

Scotty drives through the rain. He passes a road sign that reads Route 66 East, and then another which reads, Maple Grove 3 miles.

103   EXT. VIVIAN'S HOUSE - LATER   103

Scotty pulls up in front of Vivian's house and sees the "For Sale" sign. He jumps out of the car and knocks on the front door, but no one answers. He looks in the windows and sees an empty house.

He sloshes into the front yard and pulls down the "For Sale" sign. He stands there, thinking, for a minute in the rain, and then tosses the sign into the back of his car and drives off.

104   EXT. MOTEL COFFEE SHOP - MOMENTS LATER   104

Scotty parks out front and runs inside. The rain has stopped and the sky is clearing.

105   INT. MOTEL COFFEE SHOP   105

Scotty enters, soaked from head to toe with a expression of profound confusion. Lorraine is surprised to see him.

                         SCOTTY
                Where's Vivian!?

                         LORRAINE
                Oh, Scotty! She went to St. Louis.
                She left yesterday. She got worried
                when you didn't come back. I told
                her to wait. I told her to call
                you.

                         SCOTTY
                      (in exasperation)
                Why didn't she call me!?

Lorraine runs out from behind the counter and hugs him with tears in her eyes.

                         LORRAINE
                She did! She said you were too busy
                to talk to her.

                                              (CONTINUED)

                         SCOTTY
              What! I didn't get any call!

Scotty sits down at the counter. He is heart broken.

                         SCOTTY (CONT'D)
              Lorraine!

He slides a small jewelry box across the counter. Lorraine
opens it to find an engagement ring.

                         SCOTTY (CONT'D)
              I wanted to surprise her. I bought
              that the day after we met.

                         LORRAINE
              Oh, Scotty.

                         SCOTTY
              Do you know where she is? I'll go
              to St. Louis.

Lorraine shakes her head.

                         VIVIAN
              She said she'd call in a couple days.

Scotty is bewildered and just nods. Eddie enters and a broad
grin crosses his face. He runs over to Scotty.

                         EDDIE
              Hey, Mr. Scott you're back!
                 (a beat)
              You're all wet!

Eddie's greeting brings a weak smile to Scotty's face. Eddie
sees his mother's tears.

                         EDDIE (CONT'D)
              Everything OK?

                         SCOTTY
                 (confidently)
              Everything is going to be just fine.

He rubs the top of Eddie's head and exits.

106   INT. MAPLE GROVE GAS STATION - GARAGE - MOMENTS LATER   106

Ed is cleaning off the workbench. Scotty enters.

                         ED
              Glad to see ya back! You're all
              wet.

Dejected, Scotty drops down on a stool.

                    ED (CONT'D)
          You heard?

Scotty nods.

                    SCOTTY
          How do I get her back, Ed?

                    ED
          Life's a funny thing sometimes.
          Seems you two went in opposite
          directions lookin' for the same thing.

                    SCOTTY
          Doesn't help, Ed.

                    ED
          Boy, there's all kinds of hurt in
          this world. When you rammed that
          plane, you saw it comin'. Back in
          '46 she never did, and it left a
          scar. She won't let that happen
          again.

Scotty listens without responding.

                    ED (CONT'D)
          She wants to believe in you. Give
          'er a reason.

A bewildered Scotty considers Ed's words. Ed adds some
encouragement.

                    ED (CONT'D)
          I figure your the kind of man who
          can find a way.

Ed pats Scotty on the shoulder.

107   INT. VIVIAN'S BAKE SHOP - MORNING - NEXT DAY   107

Clarice is working behind the counter when Scotty enters
dressed in his khaki flying outfit and leather jacket.

Clarice is surprised to see him.

                    CLARICE
          Mr. Scott!

                    SCOTTY
          Good morning Clarice. Do you know
          where Vivian is?

                                        (CONTINUED)

She shakes her head in bewilderment.

                    CLARICE
          St. Louis. I would tell you if I
          knew more.

Scotty wears a look of disappointment.

                    CLARICE (CONT'D)
          Wait! Maybe Bryce knows.

Scotty sneers.

                    SCOTTY
          Bryce! Thank you.

He turns to leave.

                    CLARICE
               (pleading)
          You're going after her, aren't you?

Scotty glances at Clarice.

                    SCOTTY
          Count on it!

Clarice smiles and he exits.

108 EXT. MAPLE GROVE SAVINGS AND LOAN - MAIN STREET - MOMENTS   108
     LATER

Scotty enters the small white-washed brick building.

109 INT. MAPLE GROVE SAVINGS AND LOAN   109

Scotty marches past the teller windows and directly to Bryce's
desk. Bryce rises and backs away fearing a confrontation.
Scotty presses in close, face to face.

                    SCOTTY
               (firmly)
          Bryce, I'm going to ask you this
          nicely, only once. Where is Vivian?

Bryce backs away shaking his head.

                    BRYCE
          I only know St. Louis. She didn't
          tell me where she was going to stay.

Bryce holds his hands in front of him in a surrender position.
Scotty glares at him deciding whether or not to believe him.

Scotty storms out of the bank.

110   EXT. MORRIS FARM - MOMENTS LATER   110

The yellow and blue AT-6 Texan lifts off the field and climbs
sharply, high into the clear blue sky with Scotty at the
controls. He performs a barrel roll and banks to the
southwest towards St. Louis.

111   EXT. SKY OVER THE CITY OF ST. LOUIS   111

At 200 mph Scotty makes the trip from Maple Grove to St.
Louis in about 20 minutes. He circles high over the city.

112   EXT. ST. LOUIS CITY STREET   112

It's a new day. Vivian resumes her quest with a new outfit
and her portfolio in hand. She hears the HUMMM of an airplane
overhead as she walks down the street and looks up, but does
not see it.

She shuffles through the revolving doors of another office
building.

113   INT. AT-6 COCKPIT   113

Scotty doesn't know what he is looking for, but suddenly, a
look of inspiration colors his face.

114   EXT. SKY OVER THE CITY OF ST. LOUIS   114

Scotty pulls the plane into a steep climb soaring high into
the sky and performs a loop. At the bottom of the loop he
rolls the plane in a series of barrel rolls. He repeats the
maneuver.

115   INT. AT-6 COCKPIT   115

He checks his watch and taps the fuel gauge. Scotty circles
the city once more, and then, reluctantly, heads for home.

116   EXT. SKY OVER THE CITY OF ST. LOUIS   116

The AT-6 heads away from the city and disappears in the
distance.

117   INT. OFFICES OF MIDWAY CONFECTIONARY COMPANY   117

Vivian enters and approaches the RECEPTIONIST2.

                    RECEPTIONIST2
          Can I help you?

                    VIVIAN
          Vivian Donnelly to see Mr. Wallace,
          please.

                                        (CONTINUED)

                    RECEPTIONIST2
          Yes, he's expecting you. I'll let
          him know you're here. Please, have
          a seat.

Vivian turns to take a seat and notices the model of an
aircraft carrier on a side table.

She is drawn to it. She stands looking it over deep in
thought. WALLACE appears behind her.

                    WALLACE
          It's the USS Hornet. A fine ship.
          I served on her during the war.

                    VIVIAN
          Oh, good morning. Were you a pilot?

                    WALLACE
          Me? No. Pilots were a special breed
          of man.

She smiles and nods.

                    WALLACE (CONT'D)
          Well, Miss Donnelly, we've been
          looking forward to meeting with you.
          Please come in.

Vivian takes one last look at the model, and then enters
Wallace's office.

118 EXT. SKIES OVER MAPLE GROVE   118

Scotty buzzes Vivian's house and flies off into the sky.

119 INT. HOTEL HALLWAY - ST. LOUIS - EVENING   119

Vivian walks down the hallway escorted by a handsome young
BUSINESSMAN sharply dressed in a business suit. She carries
her portfolio and a 9x12 manila envelope. She stops at room
111 and takes out her key.

                    BUSINESSMAN
          Here you are Miss Donnelly, safe and
          sound.

                    VIVIAN
          Thank you, Frank.

She opens the door. The Businessman lingers.

                    BUSINESSMAN
          By the way, that was an excellent
          presentation you gave today.

                                        (CONTINUED)

                         VIVIAN
          Thank you.

She starts to enter.

                         BUSINESSMAN
          So, Miss Donnelly, would you be
          interested in a late dinner?

                         VIVIAN
          Oh, maybe another time. I have some
          work to do.

                         BUSINESSMAN
          Oh, OK. Well, I'm going back to the
          office. Call me if you change your
          mind.

Vivian smiles, nods politely and then enters her room.

120   INT. HOTEL ROOM IN ST. LOUIS - EVENING   120

Vivian enters and flips on the lights. She places the
portfolio and envelope on a table, and then goes over to the
window. She can see the lights of Busch Stadium in the
distance. There is heartbreak in her eyes.

She rambles restlessly around the room. She goes back to
the table and runs her fingers over the envelope. She sits,
pulls out some papers and shuffles through them. She begins
to study one, but can't seem to focus.

She sits on the bed, half-heartedly picks up the phone and
DIALS.

121   INT. BUSINESSMAN'S CAR - LATER   121

Vivian appears uneasy as the Businessman drives.

                         BUSINESSMAN
          Glad you changed your mind. This'll
          be better than sitting alone in a
          hotel room.

Vivian nods half-heartedly. He notices her apprehension and
turns on the RADIO.

                         BUSINESSMAN (CONT'D)
          Maybe some music.

The MUSIC fades out and a radio ANNOUNCER takes to the air.

                                                    (CONTINUED)

                    ANNOUNCER
          We can report the case of the mystery
          flyer has been solved! Earlier today
          the city of St. Louis was treated to
          a daring display of aerial acrobatics
          as Navy veteran and Medal of Honor
          winner, Lt. Richard Scott, performed
          loops, rolls and dives high above
          the city in an old World War 2
          fighter.

Vivian's interest is piqued. Businessman attempts to change
the channel, but Vivian stops him.

                    ANNOUNCER (CONT'D)
          Lt. Scott won the medal of honor
          when he rammed his plane into a
          Japanese Kamikaze to protect his
          shipmates. When reporters caught up
          with him in the little town of Maple
          Grove and asked why the audacious
          aerial acrobatics, Lt. Scott replied,
          "I wanted a friend to know I was
          back and would be waiting for her".
          Well, hopefully message received
          Lieutenant, and thank you for your
          service.

                    BUSINESSMAN
          Imagine that.

Vivian's face brightens for a moment, but then her expression
becomes more pensive.

                    VIVIAN
          I'm sorry, Frank. Maybe this wasn't
          such a good idea. Would you please
          take me back to my hotel?

Businessman scowls and nods.

122 INT. CABIN #7 - BEDROOM   122

A somber Scotty packs his duffel bag. He finishes and lays
on the bed, staring up at the ceiling contemplating his next
move.

123 INT. MOTEL COFFEE SHOP - MORNING - NEXT DAY   123

Scotty sits at the counter looking forlorn. His duffel bag
sits by his side. Lorraine stands behind the counter.

                    SCOTTY
          It's been three days. I'm going to
          St. Louis!

                                        (CONTINUED)

Someone enters. Scotty turns and sees Vivian. His eyes
reflect a mixture of disbelief and joy.

                    VIVIAN
          Where you headed, sailor?

                    SCOTTY
          I'm going to find my friend. I miss
          her terribly and I'm afraid I lost
          her when I went away. But no matter
          what it takes, I'm going to find
          her, and tell her how I feel.

Vivian sits next to Scotty.

                    VIVIAN
          Do I know her?

                    SCOTTY
          She's a self-assured young woman
          with sparkling blue eyes and a smile
          that lights up all outdoors. My
          life is empty without her.

Vivian's eyes fill. Lorraine clutches her chest with tears
in her eyes.

                    SCOTTY (CONT'D)
          Why are you here?

                    VIVIAN
          I'm looking for my friend. I miss
          him terribly. I was foolish and ran
          away to find something I already
          had. I just hope he'll forgive me.

Vivian takes Scotty's hand.

                    VIVIAN (CONT'D)
          He's a smalltown guy who likes
          baseball and cars, and makes me feel
          special whenever I'm around him.
               (a beat)
          Maybe I can help you find your friend?

Scotty beams.

                    SCOTTY
          It would make it a lot easier.

Vivian and Scotty embrace. She kisses him passionately just
as Eddie enters.

                    EDDIE
          Oh, yuck, not again!

                                        (CONTINUED)

Vivian grabs Eddie and hugs him.

                    SCOTTY
               (to Vivian)
          Well?

Vivian hands him a business card.

INSERT CARD

which reads, AUNT VIVIAN'S BAKE SHOPS, Headquarters, Maple
Grove, Illinois, MA 9-7777.

BACK TO SCENE

                    VIVIAN
               (beaming)
          I got them to agree to trying 3 shops
          here in the midwest, and I can work
          from my shop here in Maple Grove!

Lorraine runs around the counter and hugs her.

                    LORRAINE
               (to Vivian)
          Did you hear about Scott Enterprises
          new office in St. Louis?

Vivian looks at Scotty for confirmation. He nods.

                    VIVIAN
          Oh, Lorraine, I have no place to
          stay! My house has already been
          sold.

Scotty shakes his head. He hands her the keys to the house
and the jewelry box. He gets down on one knee and takes her
hand.

                    SCOTTY
          Vivian, I love you. Will you share
          it with me?

She opens the box. Vivian is too choked to speak. She nods,
and hugs Scotty again.

124 EXT. VIVIAN'S HOUSE - DAY   124

Lorraine drives Scotty's old car down the road to Vivian's
house with Ed riding beside her. She pulls into Vivian's
driveway behind two new cars.

                                        (CONTINUED)

Scotty, Vivian, and Eddie play ball in the back yard. The J-5A Piper Cub airplane sits outside a small hangar in the field behind the house.

                                        FADE OUT: